HOUSE OF SECRETS

Eve Sutherland returns to Australia to reconcile with her Aunt Lucy, but is too late. Her Aunt has died, and Sam Easton, her childhood hero, condemns her for ignoring Lucy during her long illness. Bereft, she settles into the old family home, but finds no peace, for it whispers of unresolved conflicts. Can she stay on, or does her future lay in a return to the anonymity of England? Before she can decide, her destiny is sealed by a series of disturbing events.

JO JAMES

HOUSE OF SECRETS

Complete and Unabridged

LINFORD
Leicester

First published in Great Britain in 1998

First Linford Edition
published 2005

British Library CIP Data

James, Jo
    House of secrets.—Large print ed.—
Linford romance library
1. Love stories
2. Large type books
I. Title
823.9'2 [F]

ISBN 1–84395–702–7

Published by
F. A. Thorpe (Publishing)
Anstey, Leicestershire
Set by Words & Graphics Ltd.
Anstey, Leicestershire
Printed and bound in Great Britain by
T. J. International Ltd., Padstow, Cornwall

This book is printed on acid-free paper

1

The moment Eve stepped on to the veranda of the old homestead, she heard the whispers. Clapping her hands to her ears, her eyes glazed with tears. Would she ever be able to forget that awful afternoon so long ago?

She'd come home to Australia to make peace with her aunt, to tell her she'd never stopped loving her, but already the memories threatened to ambush her. As the whispers faded, an eerie hush came over the sundrenched countryside. Eve shivered, though it must have been around one hundred degrees, and forced herself to the basket of fuchsia which hung from a veranda post.

She slid her fingers into it, and when they touched the cool, metal object, her tension eased. Lucy still hid the front door key in the plant because she knew that one day her niece would return. Eve was about to place it in the lock when a deep voice cut into the silence.

'What on earth do you think you're doing?'

Spinning round, she almost fell over her suitcases. In a halo of sunshine, a tall, dark figure materialised out of the backdrop of bushes and gum trees and strode towards her. Two black Labradors bounded at his side.

'Excuse me?' she shrilled, alarmed, as he drew nearer eyes hidden behind dark glasses.

There was something about him, his features, silhouetted against a rainbow of sunshine, which sent a tremor of fear through Eve. She decided to get inside without delay, and turned back to slot the key in the lock. But the hard-edged voice assailed her again.

'Oh, no, you don't, lady. You're not getting into this house.'

Her heartbeat quickened as she faced him.

'And who's going to stop me?'

What a homecoming! Only an hour or so back in Australia and a dark stranger was accusing her of trespassing on her family property! There was a wildness, a ruthlessness etched into the granite-like features. If only he'd remove his dark glasses and she could see his eyes, it might help her decide. Though her thoughts ran helter-skelter, she stared back at him, determined he should not know he'd thoroughly unnerved her.

'I'll stop you if I have to. Squatters aren't welcome in these parts.'

She laughed in disbelief.

'Do I really look like a squatter? Would a squatter have all this luggage.'

'She might, if she were planning to move her friends in with her.'

'Look, whoever you are, I've just got off a plane from England. I'm hot and tired, and I can do without this aggravation. Now, will you leave quietly, or do I call the police?'

The mid-February sun was slowly setting and across the western horizon vivid colours promised another very hot tomorrow. She faced him, her eyes blazing.

'Go ahead,' he mocked, 'call them. We'll soon see who's right.'

His white teeth flashed in the fading sunlight. Now it became clear. He was disturbed. He ought to be humoured. She softened her tone.

'I'm sorry, but it looks as if you've come to the wrong property. This is my aunt's place.'

She turned back to the door, anxious to get inside quickly, but the key in the lock refused to turn. Behind her, she heard him move closer.

'Your aunt's place, eh?'

Even above the pounding of her heart, his voice sounded different, lighter. She gave the key another twist. He laughed.

'You're wasting your time.'

Stay cool, she urged herself, as she spun round to challenge him again. He was standing with his arms folded, his long legs planted possessively in the driveway, as if he owned the land, as if he owned the world. Uncertainty overcame Eve. Had the taxi driver dropped her at the wrong property? She glanced about her and was relieved to find that though the garden was a little overgrown, the trees taller, this was indeed Banksia Valley.

Who, in heaven's name, was this trespasser of the dark, intimidating posture and dogs who sat in supplication at his heels? Studiously, he removed his dark glasses and for the first time their eyes locked. His were not the eyes of a deranged person. In fact, she had the oddest feeling that she'd met him before.

'Eve?' he said lightly, before pausing. 'You really don't recognise me?'

Astonished, she wrinkled her brow.

'Should I?'

'I have to admit I hadn't the foggiest who you were at first. But when you said this was your aunt's place . . . I'm Sam Easton.'

She stared at the man who stood

before her, hardly able to comprehend what he said.

'You can't mean Sam Easton from Weetangera? Why didn't you say so instead of leading me on?'

Her relief was tinged with annoyance.

'I didn't recognise you. You look so different, so sophisticated.'

'Well, do I get an apology for being called a squatter?'

She was half-joking, trying to ease the tension, trying to equate the aggressive, adult Mr Easton with her boyhood idol. His lips parted, his white even teeth glinted.

'So I got it wrong, but I should have guessed squatters don't usually have posh English accents. It's been, what . . . ten, fifteen years? Last time I saw you, you were a tubby, little kid with freckles and braces on your teeth.'

He wiped his brow theatrically with the back of his large hand, and turned to the dogs.

'Can you believe that fellas? Evie Sutherland has grown into a willowy young lady. I suppose there's no mistake.'

The dogs pranced and barked, their tails wagging effusively. A cloud of dust hung in the warm air.

'I hope the dogs see the joke. I certainly don't,' she snapped wearily.

'So the globe-trotting adventuress has finally deigned to come home.'

'I beg your pardon?'

Eve was furious, disappointed. The boy of her girlhood dreams, her young Adonis, the rangy, serious youth had grown tall, lean and muscled, outrageously attractive in a dark, Gothic kind of way — but unpardonably rude and she'd had enough.

'I'm going inside. I'm jetlagged and desperate for a cool drink, so if you'll excuse me. Perhaps we'll meet again soon.'

As she struggled to turn the key, he gentled her aside.

'Here, let me.'

Producing a key from the pocket of his jeans, he unlocked the door, and gestured her into the hallway.

'After you, madam.'

'Why have you got a key to this house?' she demanded.

'I'm your aunt's lawyer. I advised her to have the locks changed when she went into hospital. Apparently she'd handed out keys to various people over the years. Obviously she forgot to mention the one in the hanging basket.'

'If you wouldn't mind putting it on the hallstand, I'll say good-night. Thank you for looking after my aunt's affairs. If you tell me which hospital she's in, I'll ring them.'

'I'm not leaving. I have something important to tell you. Sorry.'

Sorry? He didn't sound it, but she was too tired to argue. Taking several quick paces into the quiet, dark house, suddenly Eve felt a frisson of fear tingle up her spine. The whispering began again. It appeared to come from the upstairs bedroom.

She froze, unable to walk back into

the house, which had been filled with happiness until that awful day in July, her seventeenth birthday. Sam's hand fell on to her shoulder. She jumped, and turning abruptly found herself being held at length in his arms.

Her wide eyes flashed him an appeal, but as suddenly as she had felt the security of his touch, she realised the danger of being close to him. Her face grew hot, colour burned down into her neck. She was glad of the half-light with its secretive shadows.

'Eve, are you scared of the dark? We can soon fix that.'

He touched a wall switch, which plunged the hall into light, but, she thought, Sam mustn't know what had scared her.

'It's been so long since I was in this house.'

'So you're glad to have me around, eh? First I let you in and now I'm protecting you from the dark.'

'I'm a very resourceful person. I'd have broken a window and got in if necessary, and I don't need anyone's protection.'

Her second protest sounded a bit hollow.

'If you're the same little Evie I used to know, I go along with that.'

He grinned. It lifted her spirits, but as she moved along the cool passageway, once more the memories overcame her. Running her hand across her brow, she forced her leaden feet to the open living area and kitchen. There, she threw her bag on to the table, and from an overhead cupboard, reached for a glass, turned on the tap and ran water into it.

After a few quick swallows, she glanced around her. The room looked lived in, was achingly familiar. Had she really been gone all those years? She listened, almost expecting her aunt to call, 'Eve, you're home.'

Instead Sam shouted from the hallway, 'I'll put your cases in the bedroom and then I'll take the dogs back to Weetangera. I won't be long.'

'We can talk in the morning. Don't put yourself out by coming back. I'm fine,' she called, but there was no response.

With all the drama, Sam hadn't given her the name of the hospital her aunt was in. She found the notebook sitting, as it always had, beside the phone, and thumbed through it. A hospital in the adjoining district was listed so she dialled the number, but they had no patient named Lucy Attwood. She could ring Sam, but as he sounded definite about coming back, she waited.

The house grew alarmingly silent. She ran her hand along the mohair rug which lay over the back of a comfortable chair. Lucy's, she thought. Everything reminded her of the aunt she loved, but had turned her back on. The aunt, whose explanation she had refused to listen to. Tomorrow she would see her, hold her hand, tell her she'd take care of her while she was ill. Tomorrow, everything would be different.

11

She wandered across to the china cabinet. The Royal Doulton dinner set, which Lucy had promised her when she married, still sat there on display. If she wasn't careful, she'd bring on an outbreak of tears. Fix your mind on unpacking, settling in, anything to stem the emptiness in your heart, she told herself, but it was impossible. Her aunt was dying. At least she could be with her when it happened.

When Sam called from the front door, 'I'm back,' she felt irritatingly relieved that she was no longer alone in the house.

'You look all in. Would you like a cup of tea?' he asked, almost kindly.

'I'd love one, but there won't be anything in the house.'

'No worries.'

Astonished, she watched him fill the kettle, take down a jar of tea bags, biscuits and sugar from a cupboard.

'I'm puzzled. Who got in these supplies?' she asked.

'Can't you guess?'

'I'm too tired for guessing games, Sam.'

'I'll get that cup of tea. You sit down,' he said, and was back at the stove, pouring water into the mugs. 'Milk and sugar?'

'Weak black,' she said, sinking into the sofa. 'Why is it you never really answer my questions? You've got it down to an art form, Sam. I'm still waiting to know what hospital my aunt's in.'

He handed her a mug of tea. She clasped both hands about it and watched him sit in the chair opposite.

'Ah, yes. Unfortunately, there's no easy way to tell you this. Your aunt died, Eve.'

'Lucy died? It can't be,' she cried out. 'When, what happened?'

Her voice trailed off in a whisper. Tears stung behind her eyes, and when he spoke, his voice had softened slightly.

'Last week. Why didn't you let my firm know your plans?' But then the sarcasm was back. 'We'd have rolled out the red carpet for the early return of the prodigal niece. Lucy needed you.'

'I can't take this in,' she said, brushing at the tears she couldn't control.

'Thank goodness your aunt will never know her only living relative didn't even bother to show up for her funeral.'

Eve gave an anguished cry.

'I didn't know. You're her legal representative. Why didn't you get in touch with me?'

If she couldn't say goodbye to her aunt, how would she be able to make peace with her?

'We tried, believe me, many times. You were uncontactable.'

'You must have known I'd come back. Why didn't you postpone the funeral? I could at least have seen Lucy, touched her, talked to her.'

'How long did you expect us to wait? Your aunt tried to get in touch with you in England for months. You didn't answer any of her letters. She wanted to see you before she died, not afterwards. She told me there were things she needed to explain, things you didn't understand.'

Eve came quickly to her feet, her eyes fiery.

'I received no letters from Lucy. If I had, I'd have been back here in a flash. I came as soon as I got the solicitor's message.'

'Not one letter? After she knew she was dying, she was desperate to contact you. I posted many of the letters myself, so I know she wrote them, but she heard nothing. Not a phone call, not even a postcard. How could you have been so cold-hearted?'

Eve lashed out.

'If you're trying to make me feel guilty, you're not succeeding. I don't know what happened to the letters. I do know I didn't receive them. My conscience is clear on that point.'

'Come on, Eve. This is me you're talking to, not some half-baked kid. It's obvious you didn't care about your aunt. You were living the high life in Europe, having a good time. Why would you give a second thought to Lucy back home in little old Oz?'

'It must be lonely up there on the high moral ground, but may I remind you, you're not family and you're not my conscience. So if you wouldn't mind leaving now, I'll call your office tomorrow for an appointment to discuss my aunt's affairs. For now, I'll see you out.'

Seething, she willed herself to the door, though her legs felt decidedly spongy. He didn't follow as she had hoped.

'Please go, I want to be alone. I don't want you here.'

Her voice rose as she spun round. He was standing so unnervingly close that the twilight filtering through the window picked up the day's growth emerging along his strong jaw line.

'Sit down, Eve,' he said and in one quick movement, he grasped her arm. She drew in her breath, suspecting, in mild panic, that he was about to lean down and steal a kiss. And suddenly he became young Sam, her childhood idol, the boy she'd watched on school holidays from her spying tree, stealing kisses from girls much older than herself. And she wondered, as she had then, how those lips would feel upon hers.

Eve had steeled herself against affairs of the heart, after that terrible experience here at Banksia Valley so many years ago, yet suddenly her body was sending bewildering sensual messages. She took a gulp of air and forced herself to step back from her crazy feelings. Stay away from him, her mind signalled. Stay away, stay away, Sam Easton, her wide, fiery eyes warned him.

He laughed softly in the half light, a sorcerer, she suspected, who could see into her mind.

'We have to talk. Besides, I wouldn't dream of leaving you in the lurch.'

His warm breath feathered along her

cheekbones, as he withdrew his hold on her. She leaned against the door for support, her breathing shallow, but ready to ward him off if he moved closer.

'Don't flatter yourself, Sam Easton. There's nothing I need from you tonight, or any . . . '

She let the sentence hang there, realising in a rush that in the end they'd have to call a truce, as he was her aunt's lawyer. But tomorrow she would transfer Lucy's affairs into the hands of another lawyer so that the estate could be settled quickly, and she was free to return to her job in Europe.

Originally, she'd planned to stay home with her aunt, perhaps perma-nently if they could re-establish their loving relationship. But now Lucy was gone, and with her the chance to put the unhappy memories behind them both. If only she'd received Lucy's letters. If only he were different. If only she could talk to him, because right now she needed someone in whom she could confide. But the adult Sam Easton was a bitter disappointment. No, that wasn't a strong enough word. He'd turned out to be an unpleasant bully with a rolled-gold ego.

'You'd better sit down, Eve. I have one other piece of news you're not going to like.'

'Nothing can be worse than hearing that Lucy has gone, that I won't ever see her again.'

An empty feeling settled in her stomach. She walked away from him, back into the kitchen. Lucy had given her the love and care denied her by a mother who preferred accompanying her husband on business trips to domesticity, and now she was gone. Eve slumped back into the sofa. He snapped his fingers in front of her.

'Hey, are you listening?'

'Yes,' she nodded absently.

'You're going to hear this, whether you like it or not.'

'Go away, Sam Easton. Go away. If I never see you again it will be too soon.'

19

'Listen to me, Eve. I was hoping you'd realise, but I'm living here. Your aunt gave me a six months' lease on the place.'

Suddenly Eve was listening. She was on her feet, her hands on her hips.

'Tell me I'm dreaming, or jetlagged, anything except that you're living here! In this house?'

'I'd like to oblige, but I never lie.'

'Why, when you have a perfectly good house on the adjoining property, are you living here?'

2

Sam was angry. How could Eve walk back into Lucy's house and assume possession of it after virtually ignoring her aunt all these years? How could he allow himself to notice her beautiful fair hair shimmering in the light, the blue in her eyes shifting with the currents of her emotions. He fought back the images. It wasn't the right time to tell her everything. She was clearly exhausted. It would have to wait until tomorrow.

For now, he said, 'Weetangera's being refurbished. We're extending the wine-making facilities and turning the place into a bed and breakfast, and I needed somewhere handy to stay during the major construction work. Lucy suggested I move in here. It helped me and it meant I could look after the place while she was in hospital.'

'Why on earth would you start on the building when it's grape-picking time? Not very good scheduling for a man who puts himself up as a business whizz.'

Her knowledge surprised him, and her tone of voice irritated him. He tilted his head.

'I had no choice. Someone threw a spanner in the works and held things up earlier. We lost valuable time.'

'You mean someone was game enough to stand in your way? I'm sure you soon ran him down with your steam-rolling tactics.'

She seemed determined to be difficult. He blamed himself for his aggression at their meeting.

'If my presence in the house disturbs you, I'll move into the bungalow.'

'Not at all.'

'You understand I'll be here for months.'

'Months!'

Now she sounded alarmed. He wished he hadn't been so forthcoming.

'Probably. It's a big job.'

'I take it you're using my old room at the back of the kitchen.'

'No. It gets very hot out there under the iron roof this time of year. I'm upstairs, but if you want me to keep my distance, it's not a problem. I can move down here.'

'One night won't matter. We can discuss your arrangements to move out altogether tomorrow,' she said dismissively.

She still hadn't got it. He wasn't leaving. Legally she couldn't make him.

'And now, if you'll excuse me,' she went on, 'I'm going to bed.'

'I put your luggage in Lucy's room, by the way,' he said. 'I presumed you'd want the best room in the house.'

To his surprise, she shuddered noticeably.

'Lucy's room? You presumed wrong. I'd prefer my own room, thank you, for old time's sake.'

Surely she wasn't afraid of sleeping in the room next to his? Logic told him there was more than that behind her declaration; so did her tenseness.

'Look, if you'd feel happier, I'll move downstairs. You only have to say so. It's no big deal.'

'Don't put yourself out. I loved my little room.'

Her lips curved in an apology for a smile. Obviously there was no joy in her heart.

'It wouldn't surprise me if my old teddy bear and my wall posters are still in there.'

Her voice softened almost to a whisper.

Women, he swore under his breath, before adding in a voice she could hear, 'I'll bring down your cases. Turn on the fan. You'll boil under the iron roofing.'

'I'm not helpless. I'll get them,' she snapped, as if he'd challenged her capabilities. 'And I do remember the iron roofing. It was my room.'

Huh, he thought, but you forgot it for years.

'Damn it, you're worn out. I'll get

your bags,' he growled and hastened up the stairs before she could protest any further.

Sam had selective memories of Eve as a child. She'd been much too young to tag along with him, his brother and mates, as they explored their properties on school holidays, and sat at the dam yarning and skimming pebbles across its water. But he liked her sunny personality, her gameness, the mischievous, sometimes secretive, smile. So different from today's Eve, with her abrasive sophistication. Meeting her again confirmed what he had already gleaned from her aunt. This woman knew exactly where she was headed and how to get there.

The most generous of women, Lucy loved her niece deeply, yet Eve had allowed her to die alone. It took a pretty self-centred person to do that. He'd become more than Lucy's solicitor over time, and during her illness, he'd visited regularly, looked after her business affairs, and always encouraged her to believe that Eve would walk through the door one day, smiling, glad to be home. Lucy had been grateful, receptive, but the sadness didn't leave her eyes when they talked of her niece.

After he delivered Eve's luggage to her room, and heard her close the door, Sam made his way back upstairs to the rear room, now his bedroom and office. Usually he immersed himself easily in this dream of turning the heavily-mortgaged family property and vineyard into a world-class tourist stop, but tonight he felt unsettled.

An hour, perhaps two, went by as he tried to concentrate, the only sounds, the sighing of roof timbers as they cooled down after the heat of the day. Suddenly, he heard a noise. Was Eve calling him? He dashed aside the plans and rose, but in the silence that followed, he told himself to get real. The last thing she would want from him was help. The sound must have come from an owl, or a koala on night manoeuvres. As he sat down, he heard the sound again. This time he clearly heard Eve call his name.

Taking the stairs two at a time, he was breathing hard when she literally ran into his arms in the dimly-lit passageway at the bottom. He folded her to him, protectively, stroking her damp hair back from her forehead. Her wide, scared eyes glinted in the half light.

'It's all right Eve, I'm here. Did you have a nightmare?'

'Sam,' she said in a thready whisper, 'there's someone prowling around outside. I woke up suddenly and I . . . ' Her voice grew stronger. 'And I . . . '

She must have realised then that he held her and she wore only a filmy nightshirt, for she dragged herself away, and glared up at him, as if somehow he'd taken advantage of her. Holding her in his arms, the perfume of her skin in his nostrils excited him, but as virile as he was, he didn't take advantage of women, especially one in this fragile state.

'If anyone was hanging around, you'd have scared them off when you shouted. Come on,' he said, tilting her chin, 'it's OK. I'm here for you.'

Her eyes grew wider. For a moment he thought she would throw herself back into his arms. Fortunately for his self-control, she didn't.

'Come upstairs and sleep in Lucy's room. I'll be next door if you have any more nightmares.'

She gazed up at him, fear and defiance in her eyes, if that were possible.

'It wasn't a nightmare! Someone is out there.'

'Eve, I'm not going to try to seduce you. You can trust me. You're very attractive, especially when you fire those large, frightened eyes in my direction, but I don't take advantage of vulnerable women.'

She laughed discordantly.

'I'm not frightened of you. There's a prowler out there. Will you please shut up and listen?'

Together they stood very still, and within seconds a loud noise erupted overhead. Eve jumped. Sam grinned.

'That's your prowler? Come with me. We'll take a look outside. There's a torch in the kitchen.'

As he retrieved the light, Eve stayed close.

'Hold my hand if you're scared.'

'I'm not that scared,' she said quickly.

'Then why bother to call me?'

He laughed quietly as they stepped into the darkness of the night.

'Could you share the joke, or is it private?'

'You'll soon see,' he replied.

Outside, it was hot and still, the moon offering no more than a finger-nail of light. Sam shone the torch ahead of him. A loud sound erupted again from the roof. Eve cried out and clutched at his arm. Sam directed the beam of light in the direction of the noise. It caught two soft, dark eyes shining back at them. He looked down at Eve.

'There's your joke — Percy Possum. You've been away from home too long if you've forgotten that a possum prowling on a tin roof can sound like someone walking in hobnail boots.'

Mesmerised briefly by the light's beam, the brushtail soon scurried off, shimmying across to the water tank, and down it's side. In the darkness, Eve dropped his arm and sighed deeply.

'I feel such a ninny. I should have realised. Thanks, Sam.'

'You'd better get back to bed,' he said abruptly. 'You must be just about wiped out.'

What he wanted to say was, 'Can we linger out here beneath the stars for a while?' What he wanted to do was hold her again, to stroke the long, blonde hair, to feel her body against his, and taste her lips. In the still, warm air, in the subdued glimmer of moonlight, he found her almost irresistible.

He pushed aside his heated thoughts and escorted her back to her room, reminding himself that though Eve

Sutherland excited him, she was self-centred, uncaring, not the type of woman he admired or liked.

Next morning, Eve felt the sun streaming in through the bay window on one bare arm and shoulder. She threw back the sheet from her body, baking in drowsy comfort. When she finally opened her eyes, the sunlight danced across the bed, a northern breeze stirred the curtains, and suddenly she remembered she was back in her own room at Banksia Valley.

Oh, no, she cried inwardly, as one by one the events of last evening crystallised in her mind. She remembered Sam say that Lucy had died last week, and he was living here. She drew the sheet to her chin, closed her eyes, hoping to wish yesterday away.

Why had he moved into the house? He'd given some vague excuse about refurbishing Weetangera but she remembered the homestead as a huge, rambling place. It stretched the imagination to believe not one part of it was

31

habitable. Whatever his reason, he'd soon be gone. She sat up abruptly, straining to hear any sounds of his presence in the house.

All was quiet, but strangely, the silence disturbed her. She began to fear she might hear the whispering again, and hastily turned on the bedside clock radio. Surprised to find it was after eleven, she swung her legs out of bed. Glancing around her, her thoughts drifted back into the past.

Lucy had the room built on to the house after Eve fell from a tree and broke her leg. She had come home from hospital, her leg in plaster, slept on the sitting-room sofa, waiting impatiently for her room to be finished. Though only six at the time, she'd loved its intimacy, a place of her very own. Her thoughts faltered. Time seemed to have stood still here. Everything looked exactly as it had when she left — the white flouncy curtains, the window seat, which doubled as a toy box, the ledge lined with dolls and bears. And yes, there sat Sebby, with one glass eye glinting at her. First, he belonged to Lucy, then he'd become Eve's friend. She picked him up.

'Do you miss her, Seb?'

Her voice stalled for seconds as she pushed the tears away. Sebby looked back blankly at her with his single eye. Anxiously she set him back on the window ledge with the playthings of her childhood. She had outlived this room, she had outlived this house. It scared her. As a chill ran up her spine, she told herself to grow up. She mustn't let her memories overwhelm her.

It was already very hot, at a guess around eighty degrees. In late January, it could climb beyond one hundred degrees for days at a time. Eve closed the windows and pulled the chintz curtains to shut out the wind and heat, and, throwing on a loose wrap, made her way to the kitchen. There, on the deal table, propped against a pottery vase, sat a note.

It read, *Call me at the office when you wake to set up a meeting. You'll find food in the fridge and pantry. Don't bother about dinner. I'll bring something home.*

The nerve of him! The tone of the note, the sweep of his signature confirmed what she already suspected of him. He ran on confidence, motoring through life with style and an exciting certainty. She felt a twist of envy. Her personal life was anything but exciting. Still, she shrugged, you can't have everything. At least her career prospects were excellent.

She re-read Sam's note. I'm damned if I'm going to let you bring home the dinner, she told herself. This is my place and I make the decisions here. Tilting her head, she resolved to prepare the meal this evening. Afterwards they'd have a serious discussion. The confident Mr Easton would be out of the house by tonight, but first she must insist on knowing the reason for his hostility towards her.

Boosted by her positive decision, she went to the fridge and poured a glass of orange juice. She ran the tip of her tongue along her dry lips after drinking it thirstily. Then she spread a wholegrain roll with generous layers of butter, cheese and tomato, and, munching it, strolled out the back door.

Little had changed. The ornamental trees were taller, the apricot and peach trees full of fruit, as were the two apples. One was the Granny Smith tree she'd fallen from all those years ago. It brought a smile to her lips. Beyond the garden, the valley stretched to the dam. Crushing the straw-yellow grass beneath her feet, she made her way down the steady slope to the water's edge. The noon heat shimmered across its surface, creating a rainbow of colour before her eyes.

Eve picked up a pebble and, crouching, sent it skimming across the water. One, two, three hops She could do better with practice. So much for Sam's constant theme that she'd forgotten what it was like to live at Banksia Valley.

As a child, Eve thought her aunt's property was a piece of paradise, and now . . . She fingered a tear from her cheek, wishing the weak and weepy feeling which kept coming over her would go away. For goodness' sake, have a really good cry. It might ease your sense of loss and guilt at not being with Lucy at the end, she implored herself.

A tree branch sighed and suddenly, Eve felt her aunt's presence beside her. Her tears began to fall. She dropped on to the grass and wept, for minutes, it seemed, until at last there were no tears left. She felt drained, and knew she had not yet finished weeping for her lost family. Wiping her eyes with the sleeve of her wrap, she grimaced. So many tears, she might have boosted the alarmingly low level of the dam.

In the heat, her wrap clung to her body as she strolled back up the hill towards the house. When she arrived at a shady garden seat, spent, she flopped into it, and yawning, stretched out her legs. As she fell asleep, her mouth curved into an impish smile. She'd thought of a way of getting Sam out of her hair. If she put a large helping of very hot chilli in his meal tonight, that could do it!

'Eve Sutherland, where the devil are you?'

She woke with a start to hear Sam's explosive demand. My goodness, what on earth was he doing back here at this hour, she mused as she stretched her stiff limbs.

'So there you are!'

She looked up to see him wearing smart, dark trousers, a white shirt and a loosely-knotted tie. He stood in the back doorway. Shading her eyes, she took a harder look. Surely this elegant man couldn't be Sam of the hip-hugging, torn, old denims, the unruly hair, the atrocious manners! She had her answer immediately. He pushed his dark glasses to the back of his head, his gaze sweeping over her.

'Still swanning around in your nightwear, I see.'

Before her stood yesterday's man, clothed today in respectability.

'Put your glasses back on if it upsets you,' she snapped, pulling her loose wrap about her and retying the sash with a tug.

He slipped the glasses farther back, ran his glance over her again.

'Did I say it upset me?'

He grinned.

'You didn't have to. Your tone said it for you. I came out for a few minutes to eat lunch, went for a stroll and fell asleep. Satisfied?'

'You've been sitting out in the hot sun without a hat? You'll probably turn that fair skin of yours into one ugly, giant freckle. You already look like a . . . '

'A squashed tomato?' she cut in. 'Thanks very much. It's just what I needed to hear.'

She hurried past him into the house.

'You finish work halfway through the afternoon, do you? Some job.'

'I don't normally leave the office this early.'

'So what's your excuse today?'

'My, my, someone's very testy again.'

'And someone is very rude and personal.'

'Why didn't you ring me? Or didn't you read my note?'

'Do you ever ask rather than tell people what to do?' she snapped.

'That depends on the person. Asking doesn't help with you. I was worried about you.'

'I don't remember saying I'd phone you.'

'I told you in the note to ring and set up an appointment. I'd prefer to talk at the office where it's formal.'

'And I'm telling you I don't respond to orders.'

He tilted his head.

'Fair enough. So why didn't you answer the phone when I called here? Damn it, the condition you were in last night, jumping at the slightest sounds in the night, anything could have happened to you.'

His dark eyes, she thought, held genuine concern. She had to be mistaken. It was a ploy to win her over, to get her to agree to him staying on, and it wouldn't succeed.

'You're exaggerating. I can take care of myself. I didn't hear the phone ring, and if you're implying that I was freaked out last night . . . '

'Eve, this is getting us nowhere. We have to talk.'

'You're right, of course. But do I have your permission to shower first and get dressed?' she said cuttingly.

'A good idea. You're not leaving much to the imagination in that wrap.'

Eve gasped. Dragging the gown more closely about her, she turned. His bouts of bluntness confused her, set her heart pounding wildly.

'After tonight I'll be able to wear exactly what I like because you won't be around. If you don't go willingly, you'll force me to get a court order.'

And swinging on her heel, she hurried to her room, her first priority to get out of his sight, away from his all-seeing gaze. Eve resented deeply his intrusion into her life, the way he'd assumed a kind of ownership of her aunt, his takeover of Banksia Valley. And yet, when he looked at her with his dark eyes, he aroused feelings in her she didn't quite know how to handle.

She prided herself on being cool and independent, but Sam confused and discomforted her. He attracted her? Physically, she had to be frank, he did. But she could never fall for an imperious bully.

3

Tilting her chin, Eve stepped under the shower spray, letting the water run down her throat and body. She tried laughing off the idea that she could lust after Sam, telling herself her occasional feelings of desire were a carry-over from the age when she'd hero-worshipped the youth. Today he was a vastly different person.

In shorts and a cool cotton top, she made her way back to the kitchen, hoping to find him there. They could no longer put off their serious discussion. The more pleasant she was, the sooner they'd come to an amicable agreement. She found him stretched out on the sofa. He, too, had changed into shorts, a dark T-shirt which accentuated the colour of his hair. He sat up, swung his legs to the floor, as she gave him a cursory nod, and crossed to the fridge to pour a glass of iced water.

'Feel cooler?' he asked, as she took a chair opposite him.

'Much,' she lied, for beads of sweat trickled down her spine.

If only he'd take his eyes off her. She curved her mouth, refocussed her attention.

'And I'm ready to talk, Sam.'

He shrugged.

'I wanted to do this officially in my office, but given the time constraints, now's as good a time as any.'

'It may seem unreasonable to you,' she began, 'but we can't both live here. I want to go through my aunt's things alone, spend time over it. Besides, people might get ideas. I know that's old-fashioned but it's how I feel. Yours is a big house. I can't believe there isn't somewhere up there that's liveable.'

'The heart's been torn out of the place. We're talking major renovations. You're welcome to see for yourself. Besides, I've got a lease on this property. I'm entitled to stay.'

'Find somewhere else locally. With your connections you could if you wanted to.'

'Nowhere as handy as this. I have to keep an eye on the building contractors and the progress of the work. All the family money is tied up in this venture.'

Unfortunately, she couldn't suppress a hollow laugh.

'Come on. The Easton family was amongst the top five hundred of Australia's wealthiest.'

'Not this year,' he said flatly.

It gave her the impression that something had happened to the Easton fortune. But she had no time to ponder this, for he continued.

'You could look for somewhere else to stay yourself. You'd be more comfortable in a motel in town, wouldn't you? One with air-conditioning, a pool. More suited to your lifestyle.'

'What on earth do you think I've been doing in Europe?'

'Visiting the opera houses and

galleries of the big cities with an entourage. Lucy mentioned you were with the diplomatic corp.'

She laughed.

'So the great man is clairvoyant? He thinks he knows how I live my life, what I like to do.'

'It would take more than a clairvoyant to read your mind.'

'If all this is about hustling me back to England so you can have the house to yourself, you're out of luck.'

She leaped to her feet, gripped the back of the chair.

'In fact, I might stay on for a few months. But first let me put you straight. In Europe, I tutor and baby-sit the children of diplomats. They and their partners visit the theatres, and parties.'

He grinned.

'I got that wrong, didn't I?'

'Along with a lot of other things, but you can't be expected to know everything about my family. You are, after all, the family solicitor, not a relative.'

He shrugged his wide shoulders.

'Family or not, I probably know your aunt better than you. We grew close during the last couple of years.'

'I doubt it.'

He didn't know what had happened in this house all those years ago. Only Eve, her parents and her aunt shared the secret, and now they were gone, no-one would ever find out.

'But I'm grateful,' she added. 'I'm sure you were very kind and caring. I should have thanked you earlier.'

Obviously he'd been good to her aunt. Such generosity she could only imagine, for to her he'd been unpleasant and occasionally offensive.

'She was a great lady. We often played cards, talked well into the night. She slept poorly.'

As he drank from his mug, Eve's eyes moved to his full, sensuous mouth.

'It's well over ten years since I've seen you,' she cut in, trying to dismiss the images of those lips, of Lucy's long, restless nights.

He nodded, glanced searchingly at her.

'That long, eh? It flashed into my mind when you walked in just now with your hair pinned up. Did you ever forgive me for chopping off your pigtails?'

She dropped into the chair and giggled.

'You remember that? Heavens, I hated those ridiculous plaits. Didn't I beg you to cut them off? Poor Lucy. My mother blamed her for letting me run wild. She swore I'd never visit Banksia Valley again.'

'So that's why I didn't see you again.'

He leaned back on the sofa, his bronzed arms folded across his expansive chest.

'I sometimes wondered what happened to the freckly kid next door.'

'Rubbish. You didn't give me a second thought. Anyway, except for the following summer, I continued to spend my school holidays here. Mother

47

relented because it suited her. She wasn't tuned into domesticity and kids. She liked to travel overseas with Dad, on his business trips, so she bundled me off to boarding school and I stayed with Lucy during the holidays.'

Eve's voice faltered and she could feel tears stinging at the back of her eyes, but she forced them away. This house kept dredging up the painful memories. In time she'd grown used to her mother's indifference. Lucy's love and affection more than compensated. She changed the subject.

'So, are you married?' she asked Sam Easton.

'Was.'

'Divorced?'

She held her breath as she waited. He nodded, his eyes clouded.

'Jemima Stewart. We were at university together. She occasionally stayed with us on holidays. Perhaps you met her.'

Eve knew all the girls who came to Weetangera during the school terms.

They seemed so grown-up, so sophisticated.

'How I envied her hour-glass figure, her long dark hair. All the boys thought her dishy. But wasn't she your brother's girlfriend then?'

'No, but Simon lusted after her.'

He made no attempt to hide the hostility in his voice.

'Your knowledge is surprisingly good for someone who wasn't around when the big parties were on,' he commented.

'Oh, but I was. I'd say you were eighteen or nineteen by then, certainly past noticing and teasing a ten-year-old with freckles. The girls you chased had figures and shapely legs.'

He threw back his head and laughed.

'So how come you think you know what I was interested in at that age?'

'Easy. There's a gum tree out front, my spying tree, I used to call it. I could see right across to Weetangera and you, Sam Easton, and that young brother of yours, spent a lot of time chasing girls around the tennis court and the

49

swimming pool during the semester breaks.'

'And . . . '

'And what?'

'Did I catch them?

Though he grinned, Eve noticed a tinge of colour sweep along his cheekbones. So Sam Easton did have some finer feelings.

'If you don't know, who would?'

She placed her empty glass on the coffee table, staring ahead of her, unsettled by the memories of those long, lonely summers watching her Adonis drift into the adult phase of his life where she was too young to follow. She'd seen a succession of beautiful, young women flirt outrageously with him, and in her naïvety, dreamed that one day the plain, little girl, turned miraculously into a beautiful princess, would meet him again.

He'd sweep her up in is arms then and they'd ride off into the sunset. What a laugh! Here she was, years later, sitting opposite him, actually living in the same house, but far from being a beautiful princess, far from taking that ride to happily ever after. Her Adonis was a myth. Sam Easton in his mid-thirties resembled more a character from a world of darkness. Thrusting the ghosts of the past behind her, she started to rise.

'Going somewhere?'

His fingers closed on her arm and she could feel her pulse throbbing a sensual rhythm. Hurriedly she pulled away, sat down again, edged her chair even farther from the sofa. Their eyes met, a muscle twitched in his face.

'You don't get off that lightly. Now it's my turn to embarrass you.'

Surprised and vaguely disappointed, she snapped, 'You've done nothing but embarrass me these last twenty four hours.'

'I can do a lot better than that.'

'Try me!'

'Can you recall how Simon and I used to watch you scale our trees to pinch fruit? You were so damned nimble, like a funny, little monkey.'

He leaned back, placed his arms behind his head, and chortled.

'Being called a funny, little monkey isn't very flattering.'

'And not very appropriate today. You've grown into a lovely woman.'

An awkward silence followed. Finally, he broke it.

'Hey, I've just remembered the day you got your knickers hooked on a branch and we happened along to help you out.'

'Sure, you just happened along.'

She searched her memory for the images, her mouth upturned, sunshine in her eyes.

'You flew at us that day, demanded we clear off in not so very nice language for a boarding school girl. When I first started visiting your aunt I half expected to find you still hooked up that tree.'

She dashed a strand of hair from her face.

'Don't remind me.'

'It was a highlight of that summer for me.'

She gave way then and together they laughed. The laughter subsided and a hush descended over the room. The silences when she was with Sam unnerved her. She felt glad when he rose, slapped her gently on the shoulder, and said, 'Come on kid. You can help me make dinner, unless you'd rather go out.'

'I intended to cook something myself but lost track of time.'

'I make a mean beef stir fry,' he said handing her vegetables from the fridge. 'Does that suit?'

'Lovely.'

She hardly dared to believe that there were at last connecting. This Sam she really liked. This Sam might after all be her Adonis. Forget it, she told herself, and began slicing into a red pepper with energy. Soon the kitchen was filled with the tangy aroma of the stir fry. They sat opposite one another, their plates full, a bottle of red wine waiting to be poured.

'One of the newest from our own winery. Let me know what you think.'

He waited, the bottle poised.

'Fill your own glass,' Eve said. 'First, a toast. To the golden summers of our childhood.'

Their wine flutes tinkled as they came together. Their glances sparkled. Eve put the glass to her lips.

'Very nice,' she commented. 'Not that I'm an authority, but I think fruity is the right word.'

'I may call it Lady Lucy.'

'She'd have liked that.'

'By the way, earlier, you didn't fully explain why it took you so long to get back.'

Eve detected a hardening of his voice. She dug her fork into her food. The last couple of nostalgic hours had simply been sugar-coating, to lull her into trusting him.

'I thought I had. Anyway, why are you so interested?'

'It's obvious, isn't it?'

'Not to me. Sam, do we have to spoil things by making questionable suggestions? I'd rather you come straight out and say what it is that's on your mind.'

'Well . . . ' he said teasingly.

'Well what?' she snapped.

Sam tilted his head.

'I told you Lucy wrote to you when she discovered she only had a short while to live.'

'Where is this leading? I told you, I didn't receive the letters.'

'Sure, but why? You didn't explain that.'

Eve shook her head.

'If I knew, I'd tell you. When I returned to my flat in London from an extended tour of Europe, I found an urgent message waiting for me saying Aunt Lucy was seriously ill and I should come home. I got the first flight I could. That's the truth.'

'So all Lucy's letters went astray?'

'Am I on trial here, counsellor?'

'You can always refuse to answer. But that in itself would be revealing.'

'I assume the re-addressed letters didn't catch me up. As I said, I was tutoring the children of Embassy staff travelling through Europe. I was away for several months, and not in one place for very long. I only arrived back in London a few days ago and found the urgent message about Lucy. I didn't know of your connection with my aunt's legal affairs then.'

'I'm a silent partner in the firm these days.'

'Do you want me to go on?'

'It's all very interesting.'

She glowered at him. His insolence determined her back into stride.

'Look, if you're not taking this seriously . . . '

'Please, I insist. Go on.'

'The message shocked me. I remember Lucy as full of life.'

A tear slipped down her cheek and she blinked furiously.

'Do I detect tears? Is your hard outer surface finally cracking?' Sam asked.

Don't let him upset you. Ignore his

rudeness, she urged herself.

She tossed back her head, defying the tears. There was so much more to tell, but all these years she'd kept her promise to her mother not to reveal the truth, and she'd honoured that promise.

'It sounds very plausible, but try to see it from my point of view. You ignored your aunt for years and then lobbed in, days after Lucy's funeral, but just in time to oversee the estate being wound up. I really think anyone would find that a bit suspicious.'

'Surely you don't think I've come home for the money! That's obscene.'

Sam rose from the table saying, 'I'm a solicitor. I look for evidence, and the evidence indicates you've only come home for Lucy's estate.'

He started packing up the dishes.

'Sit down, Sam Easton. You're going to take off your blinkers and listen to me,' Eve exclaimed angrily.

'I can spare a minute or two,' he replied with a shrug.

She pushed aside her plate, trying to calm down and be objective, though her mind was spitting and churning with anger.

'I loved my aunt, and I'm desperately sorry I wasn't here for her, but I don't need her money. Both my parents left me substantial legacies, and I have a well-paid job with good prospects.'

She looked directly at him with narrowed eyes.

'The more some people have, the more they want. It may be a cliché, but it's true,' he interjected with raised brows.

'What a cynical view you have of the world. I happen to think most people aren't motivated by money.'

He walked to the sink with dishes in hand.

'OK, so you're not here for the cash.'

No apology, no softening of the scowl on his face.

'You don't believe me, do you? From the minute I arrived, you've been antagonistic towards me. Are you always this judgmental?'

'I'm a forthright bloke, and I don't apologise for that. I call it as I see it. Understand this,' he said as he folded his arms across his chest, 'I've seen families break up over something as simple as a set of not very expensive cutlery. Money brings out the very worst in some people, and as your aunt's lawyer, it's my duty to protect her interests.'

Eve was beginning to wonder if some recent event is his life had made him so distrustful of people.

'As a solicitor, you should also know the importance of giving people a fair trial,' she countered.

'My client's interests always come first.'

'You haven't said you believe I'm not after Lucy's money.'

He straightened up.

'I believe you. How does that sound? Eve, if I seem blunt it's because I've got a lot on my mind, and your aunt's estate is one small item. I want it wound up as efficiently and as quickly as possible. I need to know how long you intend to stay.'

'When I know myself, I'll tell you.'

'I have a buyer for the property who loves the land and has offered a good price, but he wants an answer within the week. Lucy agreed verbally to the sale under certain conditions before she died, so if you can possibly put your mind to the matter and make a decision, I'd appreciate it. If it's any comfort, you'd be selling to someone your aunt trusted and approved of.'

So, he'd decided she was leaving, and that she'd sell the place. It sounded very much as if he wanted her out of the way. She gave him a withering glance.

'You won't stampede me into selling Banksia Valley.'

Originally, she'd planned to stay on to nurse her aunt, and this morning, roaming around the property, she'd decided the hard decisions could wait a day or two longer until she could think more clearly. Now he'd made her uncertain again. While he was around, privacy and peace were impossible, and yet today, when alone in the house, she felt claustrophobic, as if the walls were closing in on her. If she sold, she could put the ugly memories behind her. Sam broke into her thoughts.

'Come back to me, Eve, and tell me when I can close the deal.'

'Please don't pressure me into making any decisions. Allow me some time. I'm also still hoping you'll do the gentlemanly thing and move out.'

'I could be persuaded, if you give me the OK to sell the place.'

Eve's eyes widened.

'Mr Easton, some people might think that a form of blackmail.'

'It's a business deal. Be honest, you have no intention of keeping this property. You're deliberately holding things up to annoy me, and I can assure you it's working.'

For the first time Eve sensed

uncertainty behind Sam's confident façade.

'I said I'm not going to make a snap decision. I've only just arrived home. I'm still getting over the shock of finding Lucy's gone,' she said mildly, determined not to get impatient with him. 'I'm sure you understand.'

'But your life's back in England.'

'I'd be fascinated to learn how you know so much about my life.'

Much to her discomfort, she found herself resorting to the type of unattractive cynicism that was his speciality.

'Well, you wouldn't want to bury yourself up here.'

She tilted her head, paused, and finally asked the question which had troubled her since this conversation began.

'You seem unusually anxious for me to sell. There has to be something in it for you, Sam. What exactly?'

4

Sam forced himself to meet her gaze, though her direct question had taken him by surprise. Either he'd been too aggressive, or Eve Sutherland was very perceptive. Both, he thought. She was beautiful, smart and perceptive. In other circumstances he could have fallen for her in a big way.

Should he take the risk and tell her, in her present frame of mind, that he himself wanted to purchase Banksia Valley, that he needed the added acreage to extend his vineyard to prevent big players in the wine industry taking over his smaller family holding, now that it was heavily mortgaged? He guessed Eve would laugh in his face to pay him back for what she called his arrogance. To her it wouldn't count that Lucy had agreed to the purchase but not legitimised it before she died.

He'd really screwed up with Eve. Yes, he was justified in being mad with her for neglecting her aunt, but it had been a mistake to act so bull-headed towards her. If he wanted her signature on the sale papers, he'd better do some fence mending, and quickly.

She stood waiting, her brows raised, for his answer. For now he'd bluff his way through, and hope for a more favourable time to tell her.

'I've already explained, I've got this big project back home and I'm winding up my law practice. Your aunt's affairs are small beer compared to those, something I can get off my plate quickly with your co-operation.'

'What about your parents and Simon? Aren't they taking any responsibility at the winery these days?'

'My mother died some years back.'

'Oh, dear, how clumsy of me. Forgive me,' she murmured.

'My dad's temporarily with his sister, a few miles from here. He had a stroke a month or two back. That's another reason I'm anxious to get the work completed on the property. I want to bring him home. As for Simon? Suffice to say, little brother has given up his interest in the business and moved to the bright lights of Melbourne.'

'You must miss him. He was so popular with everyone. The one with the winning personality, as I recall.'

'Simon was always the golden boy of the family.'

Sam had no intention of talking about the brother with all the personality, who had gambled away most of his father's money.

Eve glimpsed a momentary tightening of Sam's facial muscles, a chill in his eyes, as he spoke. As a child, she'd observed how people gravitated towards Simon, but she'd never have guessed Sam envied his popular young brother. Yet, just now, he'd sounded very cynical. Certainly something connected with Simon irritated him.

She remained unconvinced that his

anxiety to finalise Lucy's estate was entirely due to more time-consuming projects. Instinct told her he held something back. Whatever, it wasn't her concern. She had her own problems with Sam. She dried the last of the dishes and hung the towel on the front of the stove.

'I suppose we're going to have to live in harmony in the house until I reach a decision. I won't even attempt to argue with your lease, after all you're the one with the law degree, but just for my edification, perhaps you'd like to explain how you managed to persuade Aunt Lucy to sign the lease for six months.'

He laughed, a harsh, unmusical sound.

'Damn it, are you suggesting anything in particular?'

Eve noted the flicker of response to her question as he looked up quickly. Suddenly a startling idea leaped to mind. He'd accused her of wanting Lucy's money. What if he'd been after her aunt's estate? He'd already indicated the Easton finances weren't good. He could easily have beguiled a sick lady with no family around to protect her. It might explain why he was so put out when she arrived back unannounced. As a matter of fact it might explain a lot of things.

'I asked you a question,' she repeated.

He laughed.

'You think I was after her money? What a load of old codswollop.'

'It must have been very inconvenient for you when I showed up.'

'Aren't you forgetting how critical I was that you didn't get here earlier?'

'How do I know you weren't putting on an act? I only have your word that Lucy wrote to me. You could have manipulated her into signing something that made it possible for you to get your hands on her assets.'

'I suppose I could have.'

'You suppose?'

She turned her fiery gaze on him. He cut in, laughing coldly.

'After the hospital bills, there's almost no money left. I was jesting, Eve.'

'So why aren't I laughing?'

Her heart did a double flip. Had he really been teasing her?

'There's the property and you want it sold in a hurry. This place would be worth something on today's market. Tell me, Sam, how many more days were there to go before you got your sticky hands on the estate?'

She glared at him, reinforcing her position by thrusting back her shoulders. Sam's steely stare bored into her.

'Didn't you hear me? You're talking emotional claptrap. I'm going to take a shower and then I'll be in my bedroom working if you have something constructive to add to the conversation. Otherwise, I'll be around tomorrow and Sunday. I'll be at the homestead. Come up. I'll be happy to show you around. Then you'll understand why I can't live there.'

With a forbidding glance, he turned

sharply and strode from the room, leaving her standing uncertainly, puzzled.

That night, Eve couldn't get to sleep. It had been a mistake to challenge Sam about the property. In her heart she knew he wasn't the kind of person who'd manipulate anyone, let alone a sick woman, who relied on him for so much. She ran her hand across her hot brow. It was so hot in this little room.

Throwing on a light gown, quietly she made her way out to the kitchen, poured a glass of soda and strolled on to the veranda. Though there wasn't a breath of wind, the air outside felt marginally cooler. His voice, a harsh whisper in the darkness, pulled her up with a start.

'Eve, don't make a sound.'

She put her hand to her mouth to close out her startled cry. In a swish and flutter of wings several bats took off from the trees nearby.

'Fruit bats?' she whispered.

'Yeah, and you can stop whispering. You've driven them from their feast on the apricot trees. Did you recognise the sounds?'

'I spent many a hot night out here as a kid watching them.'

She could see Sam's outline sitting on the edge of the veranda. She made her way towards him.

'It's awfully hot inside. Is there any danger of bush fires this year, do you think?' she asked.

'It wouldn't surprise me. We've had no decent rain now for months.'

She sat down a safe distance apart from him.

'I remember the big one at Warrandyte. It came awfully close to our area. I must have been at secondary college then. It was during the Christmas break. Dad went out on one of the fire trucks to fight it, and left behind three females, quivering with anxiety.'

She laughed.

'Poor Dad, spending the holidays in a house with so many bossy women. The Three Musquettes, he called us.'

'You were happy then?'

70

'I had a wonderful childhood. If I have any children . . . '

'Is that why you want to keep Banksia Valley? You didn't mention you were married. Lucy would have been delighted. She had no idea you planned to raise your children here.'

Eve's heart missed a beat.

'You're 'way too far ahead of me, Sam. I'm not married, and until this minute I hadn't given any thought to raising children here. I suppose the tranquillity of the evening drew the notion from my subconscious.'

'It's a nice dream. One you should hold on to.'

'Does that mean you're not going to press me to sell?'

'Naturally I'd like to go ahead with the sale, but you've persuaded me you need more time.'

'Thanks. I promise I won't keep you waiting too long for a decision. And by the way, forgive my outburst earlier. My emotions are all over the place at the moment. I don't doubt your fondness

71

for Lucy. Of course you wouldn't cheat her.'

To emphasise her contrition, she reached out and touched his arm in the darkness. His hand covered hers. It's strength set her heart pounding.

'Or you. It means a lot to me that you've recanted. You know, Eve, I have to keep reminding myself that you're the little blonde waif who used to tag around with me. Why didn't you join Simon's fan club like the rest?'

'Because I liked you better. Simon was all right, but you tolerated me. You didn't keep telling me to clear off.'

Eve swallowed. It had been more than like, especially when he grew older, but by then he'd forgotten she existed.

'You've grown into a lovely, young woman Eve. If only Lucy could have seen you when you got older.'

He removed his hand. His gaze, in the dusky tones of the evening, felt like a caress. A hint of light shone in his eyes.

'She did. I was twenty-one when I went overseas. Lucy saw me occasionally when she came to town while I was at university. We had lunch together.'

He shifted closer. His movement sent a wave of feeling through her. Anxiously she rose from the veranda, and strolled towards a garden bed, where she stooped to pick a lavender stem and breathed in its perfume. He'd created an emotional turbulence within her merely by his nearness.

The moment she knew Sam was out here in the darkness, she should have returned inside. Instead she'd allowed herself to be bewitched by the mystical romanticism of the evening air.

'How come I didn't see you around the place when you were grown up?'

He asked questions she didn't want to answer. It reminded her that there was still a lot she didn't want the adult Sam Easton to know.

'Because I stopped coming up here after my seventeenth birthday.'

That at least was true. The next part

she fabricated, to avoid further investigations.

'I made some good friends at university, and I liked living in the city and being close to the theatres,' and went on, because she wanted to close the subject, adding quickly, 'I see the lavender garden's still thriving.'

If he knew the truth. If he knew what Lucy had done . . . But that secret was forever locked inside her.

'I can't understand why you didn't give any thought to Lucy, living here alone after your mum and dad died.'

'I suppose Lucy complained about me being selfish all the time.'

'No, but she said often enough how much she longed to see you.'

'I was an only child. I needed people my own age around me,' she said.

'I don't believe you. You're not that cold-hearted. You and Lucy had a bitter falling out. Lucy wouldn't tell me why, but she said it was her fault, not yours. I'd like to understand. If you need to talk about it, Eve, I'm here. You can trust me.'

'Perhaps one day,' she said, making her way to the steps of the veranda, yawning theatrically. 'I'll see you in the morning. Good-night, Sam.'

'Good-night.'

His voice sounded distant. She could only make out his figure silhouetted against the evening light. They were as far apart as they had been when she arrived. The explicit hostility was gone, but beneath their talk still lay a simmering lack of trust. If only it could have been different.

'By the way, I didn't give you the good news.'

His voice stopped her on the second step.

'Good news? I can do with some.'

She turned back, wondering if it was good for him or her.

'I've given it a lot of thought, and I've decided to move out until you leave.'

'You're moving out?' she said, her heart beating rapidly.

'You don't sound very pleased. I

expected bells and whistles.'

'I'm pleased. Where are you going?'

'I'll set up one of the winery sheds as temporary living quarters.'

'Why the sudden change of heart? You practically waved the lease in my face earlier.'

She shivered. If he left, she'd be in the house alone at night. Did she want to be alone in this house at any time with her memories?

'I'm making you uncomfortable. Lucy wouldn't have wanted that.'

'So you're doing it for Lucy!' she snapped.

'A winery shed isn't the most comfortable place to doss in this heat. You could always talk me out of it, Eve.'

Eve pulled her lips tightly together, tossed her shoulders and said into the darkness, 'In your dreams, Sam.'

As she made her way to her bedroom, she knew she'd acted impetuously. Go straight back and ask Sam to stay on. Tell him you've been wrong from the start, her mind prompted. But pride and obstinacy prevented her.

She wondered how long she'd survive in the house on her own.

5

Eve woke next morning with a large helping of guilt. Even with the fan spinning overhead, her little room was stifling. She couldn't let Sam move into a made-over iron building in this heat when the room upstairs remained empty, even to repay him for the hard time he'd given her when she arrived. To be frank, she'd probably over-reacted to his cynicism, because she was jetlagged and upset by the news of Lucy's death.

Besides, during his absences, some-times a silence, a threatening stillness fell over the house, and, her heart on alert, she dreaded she might hear the whispers. Pulling on shorts and a top, she hurried out to the kitchen to tell him she didn't mind if he stayed. A note propped against the fruit bowl said, *At Weetangera. Will collect my things later.* S.

After a quick breakfast she changed into jeans and a pair of walking shoes, grabbed an old straw hat from the laundry, and set off on the well-travelled bush track up to Weetangera. As she strode out, she found herself looking forward to seeing the lovely old property again and enjoying the exercise. But by the time she reached the rickety old gate, erected in the barbed wire fencing between the two acreages, her pace had slowed. Pausing, she wiped her brow and replaced the catch.

The track weaved through what seemed like an eternity of vineyards. Deep purple grapes hung in luscious bunches, waiting to be picked. Eve pinched a stem from a vine and popped one into her mouth. Soon she demolished all the sweet, juicy grapes. The dryness in her throat eased.

The sounds of hammering and saws at last led her to a wide clearing, where what was left of the luxurious, ranch-styled mud-brick Easton home sat in chaos, its windows removed, its roof line being extended, some of its walls non-existent. Sam hadn't exaggerated. Workers were everywhere, pouring concrete, laying bricks, erecting frames.

She paused in the shade of an exterior wall which was being extended and called to the bricklayers working on the scaffolding.

'I'm looking for Sam Easton. Can you help me?'

Several pairs of eyes glanced up from their work to peer and grin at her.

'Yeah, the boss's working in the big shed over there.'

A thick-set man, wearing a baseball cap, pointed in a northerly direction.

'It's a fair hike, but he'll be up soon for a cuppa if you wanna wait in the shade.'

'Thanks, I'll find him.'

'Keep on the rough path. It'll get you there.'

She strode off with pep in her step but out of their sight, she paused to wipe her brow again, to get her breath and look around. She felt happy to be doing something after the last few unsettling days. She was pleased at her decision to let Sam stay, eager to tell him.

As she neared the door of the iron building, a riot of bad language poured from it. Laughing quietly, she knew she'd found her quarry. The barn-like building had no wall or doors on one side. She slipped quietly into the airless, stifling shell of iron sheeting on an expansive concrete slab floor. At one end, sat a tractor and two other harvesting vehicles. She spotted Sam near a long workbench. He had his back to her and was juggling an electric drill in one hand while searching for something on the floor.

He wore a dark singlet; his golden tan muscular arms gleamed with sweat. The denim shorts were old and frayed, the heavy elastic-sided boots scuffed at the back with age. Her heart danced at his impressive maleness.

'Where is the damned thing,' she

heard him mutter.

Smiling, she crept closer, childishly anxious to surprise him. As he scrambled amongst the litter of tools and timber shavings at his feet, obviously in a foul mood, Eve decided to make her presence known. And then her eyes lightened. There at her feet lay the drill-bit he clearly sought. It must have rolled some distance along the concrete floor. She seized it as if it were a valuable prize. Today she'd have some fun at his expense. Tapping him on the shoulder, she held the drill-bit out in front of her.

'Looking for this?'

He jerked round, sweat glistened through his hair, on his shadowed, unshaven jawline. His startled glance moved upwards to meet her eyes.

'Planning to give me a heart attack, were you?' he growled, standing and shooting out his free hand in one swift movement to retrieve the bit.

But Eve withdrew her hand before he could reach it. With considerable effort she controlled the blush which almost always accompanied an encounter with him. On her long walk up here, she'd resolved not to let her attraction to Sam dictate to her any more. She'd sown that thought in her mind, and now she put it to the test.

With a saucy smile she said, 'Temper, temper. I'm sure your mother taught you it's bad manners to snatch.'

Standing tall, his fingers still wrapped around the drill, he dwarfed her and began to erode her confidence. Her heartbeat moved up a few revs.

'The bit please, Eve. I haven't got time for games.'

The palm of his outstretched hand demanded her obedience. She hadn't come to annoy him, though silently she confessed to a ripple of pleasure at briefly having him at a disadvantage.

'Be nice,' she said.

He bared his strong, white teeth, held out his hand.

'This is being nice.'

'How sad.'

Smiling, she dropped the small metal piece into his palm. His fingers wrapped around it, and ignoring her, he inserted it into the drill. She waved her hand across his vision.

'Sam, you didn't say thank you very much, Eve.'

'Are you still here? Why?'

'Because you invited me yesterday to come up and see the renovations for myself.'

'I haven't got time now, Eve.'

'You didn't mention I'd need an appointment.'

Eve was enjoying herself. She decided to briefly delay telling him he could stay on at the Valley.

'Because I didn't think you'd bother to come. The quicker I get this job done, the sooner I'll be out of your hair. Now if you'll excuse me.'

He pressed the drill starter, the tool shrilled into action and he began urging the bit into a piece of timber, making further conversation impossible. But she hadn't finished yet. She still had to tell him of her change of heart, and all this work was for nothing. Hastening to the power point, she flicked it off and in one deft movement released the cord from its socket. The drill whinnied to a stop. He looked up sharply.

'What are you trying to prove?' he said and scowled at her angrily.

'Actually, I came to tell you something.'

She kept him guessing, playing his game, smiling.

'It can wait. Please put back the plug and clear off before I . . . '

The explosive words erupted from his throat. She'd obviously tested his patience too far. She gave an exaggerated sigh.

'Suit yourself. If you don't want to hear the good news . . . '

He dropped the drill on to a bench and in three strides stood beside her, gripping her shoulders, his fingers biting into her soft flesh.

'Don't push me, Eve. Give me the cord. You can see how busy I am, and it's damned awful hot in here or hadn't you noticed?'

Beads of sweat trickled from his forehead, sliding unhindered down the rock solid features. Through her light cotton top she felt dampness on her shoulders from his iron grasp. The nearness of his magnificent, glistening body aroused her, warmth skimmed through her body, sent up a warning signal. Retreat, she warned herself, retreat before he senses your feelings.

'I was teasing. But it seems you're better at dishing it out than you are at receiving. You can have the plug once you release me.'

His long sigh cut through the heat, fanning like a harsh desert breeze across her forehead. His fingers relaxed their hold.

'I'm sorry if I hurt you. Nothing's going right for me this morning. This isn't the time for you to be skittish at my expense.'

Standing beside the power point, she slipped the plug into the socket. Her finger poised to trigger the switch.

'Well, excuse me for trying. I was looking forward to telling you you can stay on at the Valley, but your ill-humour's taken the pleasure out of it.'

He raised dark brows.

'Say that again.'

'You can't sleep in this king-sized sauna. I won't have that on my conscience.'

She watched surprise sweep over his features, but as she pressed the switch, the drill started up, drowning out any response. He walked towards her, slowly, the piercing sound of the drill killing any attempt at conversation, until he turned it off.

'You've changed your mind? Boy, am I relieved. Are you sure about this? I want you to be one hundred per cent sure.'

'I'm sure.'

'I appreciate having me around is a pain in the neck for you. I'll try not to get in your way. Promise.'

'I'll be prepared if you transgress.'

'And I'm sorry if I was a bit rough on you just now. I've got so much on my mind.'

'No, no. I'm as much to blame. I should have realised it wasn't a good time to string you along. To make up for it, I'll cook dinner tonight.'

He smiled.

'You seem more alive today. Are you feeling happier with life?'

'I feel more positive, at least about having a house guest.'

'Instead of you cooking dinner, why don't I take you out, introduce you to one of our fine, local restaurants? Since we're going to be living in the same house for a while, it would give us a chance to do some making up.'

She surprised herself by answering, 'I think it's a good idea.'

That evening, Sam moved his upmarket sportscar smoothly down the driveway and out on to the narrow, unsealed track which led to the main road. The breeze rustled through Eve's hair, caressing it like the hands of a tender lover. To her, Sam had always been attractive. She swallowed hard, forcing herself to remember that she didn't really know this adult Sam, and there was a lot she didn't understand about him.

'Smart car,' she said coolly, attempting light conversation.

'It's garaged at your place for the time being. Feel free to use it any time. I'll give you a key.'

He turned towards her but his expression was masked by shadows.

'That's generous of you, but I wouldn't dare. What if I crashed it?'

'You do that kind of thing often? I mean it. If you need a car . . . '

'I mean it, too. In my hands, your racy little job could finish up on a lamppost. I haven't driven in ages. I don't own a vehicle. In London and on the Continent, public transport's the best way to travel.'

'On your advice, I withdraw my offer. Would you like me to hire a little runabout for you?'

'I won't be here long enough. I can get a taxi when I need to go anywhere.'

'Then you've made plans to leave?'

'No, but I should. There's nothing to hold me here.'

He swung the car into the main road. Nothing to hold her here? The words echoed in her head. She compelled herself to look out at the once-familiar countryside, now bathed in the shadows of a rising moon, but her thoughts returned to remind her Sam sat only a touch away from her. If she reached out . . . How wonderful it would be to have a man of his extraordinary strength and confidence beside her always. She uttered a quiet sigh, and relaxed deeper into the seat. She had him tonight. Why not enjoy it and let the future take care of itself?

The vehicle gathered speed and the breeze began to dance wildly through her hair, sending it streaming out behind her. Her tension and guard, too, were caught up in the rush of warm wind. A prickle of excitement rippled through her body as the car eagerly ate up the miles.

As the moon made its claim on the land, cloaking it in eerie shapes and shadows, Eve felt the headiness of adventure; daring stirred within her. Did Sam feel the way she did? She stole a glance in his direction. What really lay behind those impenetrable features, the steamy, dark eyes?

Swallowing, Eve warned herself to get her head back on straight again, to move her thoughts to where they couldn't give her pain. Start chatting, say anything mundane, try the weather.

'It's awfully dry around here,' she ventured.

'It sure is.'

She imagined his eyes glinting and felt a sudden pulse rise.

'You're deliberately misunderstanding me. You know I mean the weather,' she said lightly.

'I agreed with you. It's dry. Unless we get rain soon we may be in for another disastrous bushfire. And that's another reason why I'm glad you changed your mind about having me around the place while you're here.'

'You'll be my white knight? How romantic,' she mocked.

'Yes, if necessary. Are you going to give me a hard time again tonight?'

'Not tonight. I thought we'd called a truce.'

'Good, otherwise I'd have raised the white flag. I've had a long, hard day. A little relaxing music might set the mood for tonight.'

He turned on the tape deck. Snatches of haunting flute music carried into the night air.

''Picnic at Hanging Rock' theme music,' she murmured as her thoughts drifted back to that golden summer and she was wandering the sundrenched hills and valleys of her childhood.

Strange that the dark, more serious Sam had captured her imagination and become the focus of her romantic fantasies all those years ago, when

Simon of the golden hair had all the social attributes and winning smile. She sighed, long and silently. Sam wasn't a romantic dreamer, yearning for what could never be. His thoughts were clearly locked into the future of his much-loved property.

He would leave her behind again. It was foolish to give way to her dreams, yet she continued to allow them to intrude into her thoughts and cloud her judgement. The car accelerated on a straight stretch of road and the rushing wind whispered to her, 'Untangle your emotions and move on, too. Go back to England and safety before you get hurt.'

She pondered why she'd indulged in a haze of nostalgic nonsense, mooning over a man who didn't quite trust her, a man who believed she had callously neglected her aunt. If only she could confide in him. The moonlight, the man, the memories had affected her thinking. She stiffened her back and with it her resolve to forget her romantic notions about Sam Easton.

'I expect you're too young to have seen 'Picnic' on the big screen,' he asked casually, when the poignant notes of the music faded.

'I caught it when it was revived at a small theatre in London. I love it, of course, in case you were about to accuse me of hating everything about this country.'

She watched him heave his broad shoulders.

'I thought we'd called a truce. No more point-scoring.'

She smiled.

'It's a habit. You've been a good teacher.'

'You're breaking the rules again.'

'Sorry.' She laughed. 'Tell me about your plans for Weetangera.'

'It's a dream I've had for years, and when Dad lost his money, I put it to him and he agreed. Eve, it's going to be the best little winery and bed and breakfast in Victoria.'

'Your voice shines when you talk

about the project,' she said.

An awkward silence descended, until at last, the car pulled into a bay outside a brick homestead partly secluded by a landscape of native trees.

'This is it,' Sam said.

Eve felt relieved. At least temporarily, she could escape the uneasy, restless vibes of being so close to him.

6

'It's called 'The Cellars',' Sam commented, easing lithely from the depths of the car and hastening to open her door, but, too quick for him, by the time he arrived Eve stood on the pavement, fingering through her tumbled hair to reorganise it.

He offered his hand, but she ignored it and pushed her way along the dimly-lit brick paving, which wove through the shrubbery to the entrance. He arrived at her side but she was reluctant to stay close to him, and led the way into the restaurant. As they waited for the host to show them to a table, she thought with dismay how intimate it was with its subdued lighting and alcove tables.

'They serve excellent food and local wines here. Soon they'll have the Weetangera label on the list.'

His generous smile lit up the dusky reception area and re-affirmed how much his new business venture excited and drove him. As they were led to a dimly-lit corner table, his hand disconcertingly at her elbow, she noticed glances of envy cast in her direction by some of the women. What if the dashing Sam Easton of Weetangera were her lover? Sitting at a secluded table, the candlelight and background music creating a romantic ambience, he'd take her hand into his, ask her to marry him. They'd plan their future together, their eyes aglow with love and warmth . . .

If only . . . She blinked, lifted her lashes. Sam was holding out her chair.

'What's going on in that head of yours now?' he asked.

'I just drifted off for a minute.'

She sank gratefully into the seat for her knees had turned wobbly.

'You're tired after your walk this morning. We won't linger over the meal.'

His hand rested lightly on her arm.

Colour rushed into her cheeks. She ran her fingers over one side of her face.

'There's no hurry. Let's relax and enjoy ourselves. It's Saturday night.'

'That's the best idea you've had since you came home.'

He laughed before opening his wine list. Surreptitiously, over the rim of her menu, she watched him. Dark, curling lashes fluttered and shadowed his eyes. The candlelight between them, with its gentle radiance, softened his features. Suddenly, he looked up, as if conscious of her appraisal. Their eyes met. Alarmed, she switched her attention to the safety of the menu.

'What will you have?'

There was a smile in his voice. Eve glanced down the menu, glad of its protective shield. At last the waiter arrived with his note pad, and with relief she turned her undisciplined thoughts back to ordering. But she had lost her appetite for food.

'An entrée serving of pasta! That isn't enough,' Sam scoffed, after she'd ordered, and turning to the waiter, asked him to bring her the chilled fish chowder and herb bread first.

'And for dessert she'll have the iced Grand Marnier soufflé set in a chocolate cup. I'm trying to fatten her up. She's much too skinny.'

Eve's surprise turned to irritation as the waiter scribbled on to his pad and beat a hasty retreat.

'You make me sound like a Christmas turkey. You really are unbelievable. I suppose you admire fat, cuddly women.'

She stage-managed a smile, determined not to make a scene in public.

'I like to grasp hold of my women. You're a will o' wisp in more ways than one, Eve.'

She swallowed hard. No quick response, no cutting lines came to her aid.

'Well?' he said finally.

'Well what?' she bit back at him.

'Talk to me, Eve. There's something worrying you. Why don't you lay it on me? I know it's to do with Lucy and I might be able to help.'

It wasn't anything she could tell him. She gave a shaky laugh.

'I've already shared too much of myself with you.'

'You still think I was trying to cheat your aunt, don't you?'

His glance had turned cold with impatience. He was 'way off course from her present thoughts. It threw her a little. She didn't have a ready answer, so took a few sips of wine, searching for one.

'Trying to get Lucy's estate for yourself? No, if I thought that I wouldn't have asked you back to the house. But I have a strange feeling you're not being totally honest with me.'

The waiter arrived, saving him the need to reply, but not before she noted Sam tighten his shoulders.

Her spoon poised in one hand, she asked, 'Perhaps there's something you want to tell me, Sam?'

'I thought we came here to relax and enjoy ourselves.'

'Me, too, until you raised the subject of Lucy. You may think you know everything about her. Believe me, you don't.'

'Then tell me so I can understand.'

Tell him? How could she break her promise to her mother and tell him that Lucy, the aunt she adored, had been her father's lover?

'Eve, when she was dying, most of her pain came from not hearing from you. She had something she needed to explain to you.'

A stab of pain clutched at her heart. She'd kept her secret all these years, stored up with bitterness.

'I promised my mother not to tell anyone.'

'Your mother's dead. Lucy's dead. You can't hurt them by talking about it now.'

Eve drew in her breath but remained silent as they continued eating their meal.

'You know, don't you? Lucy told you,' she asked as they were served dessert.

'No. All she said was there'd been a family row and you refused to see or talk to her about it afterwards, that you didn't understand all the background.'

Pushing aside her plate, she snapped, 'Why do I think you're lying?'

'Because you don't trust anybody. You're wracked by uncertainty. That's why you should talk to someone. I'm offering to listen, but it doesn't have to be me. It could be a counsellor.'

'That's rich coming from someone who hasn't trusted me from the minute I appeared at Banksia Valley. I think it's time we left.'

The fact that he was right about her lack of trust in people really hurt. Wishing it weren't so, she drained the last of her wine, waited, folding and refolding her napkin, while he finished his dessert. He was down to the last spoonful when a tall man strode towards their table.

'Fancy seeing you here, old buddy.'

He slapped Sam on the back. Even in candlelight Eve found his smile wide and very winning. Sam wheeled abruptly around and leaped to his feet, his face contorted with anger.

'Fancy!' came his sharp reply. 'What are you doing in this area?'

'Is that any way to greet your little brother?'

Eve gasped. Simon Easton! But why was Sam so hostile towards him? Apparently she wasn't the only person he disliked. Perhaps the great man was just anti-social. She dismissed the thought for Sam had been generosity itself to her aunt and always spoke with affection of his father. She waited, almost holding her breath, to see what unfolded.

'Cut the bonhomie, Simon, this is me you're talking to,' Sam hissed quietly, his dark eyes narrowed.

'I'm meeting a prospective business partner here for dinner.'

Still Simon held his winning smile,

but Eve suspected he wasn't as assured as he pretended. She intervened, hoping to lighten the tension, for by now they had attracted the interest of several diners.

'Do you remember me?'

She put out her hand, her mouth curved softly in a smile.

'I believe you used to call me Freckles. Eve Sutherland.'

'Eve? No kidding!'

Simon squeezed her fingers a little too intimately for comfort.

'Are you living in these parts?'

She withdrew her hand.

'For the time being at Banksia Valley. Perhaps you know my aunt died?'

Her voice faltered. It mattered not, he wasn't listening. He really didn't remember her, she felt sure.

'We were just leaving,' Sam declared grimly.

'What a pity. We could have had a drink together. I'll call in on you, Eve, while I'm in the area if I may. Banksia Valley, you said?' Simon called as Sam ushered her away from his brother.

'I'd like that,' she had time to reply, giving Sam a determined glare. 'Any time in the next few days.'

Outside, the sultry air had cooled refreshingly. As Eve climbed into the car, her curiosity aroused, her heart quickened with interest. She had no doubt Sam's passionate distrust of his brother was due to much more than competition between two different, but stunningly attractive men.

'What was that all about?' she asked as she climbed into the car.

'You don't want to know.'

He engaged the engine with an angry flourish. The car moved jerkily on to the road. Eve suspected his thoughts were equally unsteady.

'You don't like your brother much, do you? What happened? You were such friends as boys.'

She expected him to side-track her or make excuses for his outburst. Instead he turned cold eyes upon her.

'None of this concerns you. Stay

away from Simon. He's bad news. If I hear he's called on you, I'll . . . '

The car swerved momentarily, but swiftly, skilfully he straightened it, mixing several expletives under his breath with the action.

'Yes, Sam? You'll what?'

'You wouldn't want to be around to find out.'

His voice calmed.

'I'm advising you to stay away from Simon.'

'First you tell me what to eat tonight. Now you're telling me whom I can see socially. Simon is welcome to call, unless you can convince me otherwise.'

'Then I'll have to try, but not until we get home. I need to concentrate on the road.'

'That might be wise' she said, feeling she'd won a small victory.

If she understood Sam's hostility towards his brother, she might understand a whole lot more about him.

On the veranda steps, when he let her out of the car, she turned to him.

'I'll make a cup of tea while you garage the car. We'll have it outside where it's cooler.'

She'd thought it through, hoped in a quiet, intimate ambience Sam might open up to her. As she boiled the kettle, set up the tray, she wondered what had happened to the Easton family, the nearest thing to gentry in the area when she was a child.

She found Sam sitting on the steps on the veranda, his shirt sleeves rolled up, when she turned on the outdoor lights, and carried the tea things outside. He rose quickly.

'Let me.'

He took the tray from her, set it on the table. Eve pulled her chair close, and poured the tea.

'Sit down,' she said.

He did so, almost mechanically, as if his thoughts were somewhere else.

'Sam, tell me what happened between you and your brother.'

He looked up from his tea abruptly.

'You sound as if you're enjoying this.'

'Enjoying it? I'm concerned for you. Your family used to be so close.'

'My wife left me for Simon.'

In the half-light, she watched him closely for some sign, some reaction, but to her surprise, his facial features remained impassive.

'I'm sorry, Sam. You must have been devastated.'

'I had hopes Jemmy and I could develop our own tourist winery. She'd have made an excellent hostess. But that's all in the past. It's a long while ago. I was just grateful we didn't have any children.'

He took a long gulp of his tea, rose and returned to his earlier position on the veranda steps. Eve felt he'd told her only part of the story.

'Has their marriage worked out?'

'They weren't married. Jemima didn't hang around long when she discovered Simon had no money.'

'Simon had no money? How was that?'

'He had an allowance from the family

trust, but it wasn't enough for Jemm's expensive tastes.'

'Perhaps you shouldn't be blaming Simon. She sounds as if she was a first-class schemer. She could have captivated him.'

'Oh, she did all right. But she didn't have to work that hard. He was always keen on her. I can't think now why she agreed to marry me.'

'She loved you, of course.'

He laughed harshly.

'She didn't love me. She loved the fact that I managed the family business, but when she discovered that didn't include me taking her on long overseas holidays, unlimited credit cards and so on, she reworked Simon. Somehow he must have convinced her she'd get those things from him.'

'Well, she's lost out all round, but so has Simon. Can't you patch things up with him? He is your brother and I'm sure your father would want it.'

'Dad would like nothing better.'

'Then it's OK if he calls on me? I'd

like to chat with him.'

Eve was starting to think she may be able to reunite the brothers.

'I'd prefer you didn't. He's a charmer, a manipulator. He's a lady's man. I saw the way he looked at you in the restaurant. He sees every beautiful woman as a challenge.'

'Thank you for the compliment. I don't believe it, but . . . '

'But nothing. I've told you before how attractive you are.'

'Always in a teasing tone. I didn't think you meant it.'

'You're beautiful, Eve. I find you very lovely, desirable. Most men would.'

She placed her cup to her lips and drank from it. How did she respond? What would happen if she told him she found him desirable, too, that ever since she'd arrived at Banksia Valley a few days ago he'd aroused her?

'You're very quiet.'

She could feel his gaze on her. She shifted uneasily in her chair, thought about taking the easy option and going inside.

'Enough talk about me. Shall we concentrate on you now?' he said lightly when she didn't reply.

'But you've told me so little about the present-day Sam Easton.'

'You know the necessaries.'

He stood up, leaned against the veranda railing, mildly teasing.

'I'm a good, old-fashioned country boy. What you see is what you get.'

What she saw was a man some women might literally die for. He had already managed to twist her feelings into knots.

'I doubt it. No other family secrets, no dangerous liaisons?' she teased.

'Hundreds of the latter, but X-rated. Not for your pretty ears.'

He straightened his back, laughed.

'You can't avoid it any longer. It's your turn, Eve. Won't you let me be your father confessor? Tell me what happened between you and Lucy. Nursing bitterness can turn people sour and destroy their enjoyment of life.'

Eve felt his warm gaze upon her, heard the sympathy in his voice. Did he genuinely care for her? Her doubts about Sam Easton were slowly disappearing. If she could confide the unhappy events of years ago to him, it would help rid her of the bitter memories she'd carried with her, help her put things in perspective and ease the guilt she carried for her unforgiving part in the events which happened in this house.

A voice inside urged her to break the promise she'd made to her mother. No harm could come to anyone now if she told her story. Sam had told her of his wife's duplicity. It was time for her to trust him and share her secret. She poured herself another cup of tea, wrapped her fingers around the china cup, and gazing into the night, began.

'It happened on my seventeenth birthday.'

7

'Mother and I had gone to the monthly Saturday afternoon market. I was really happy because my mother rarely spent time with me. Lucy knew that upset me. I thought that's why she and Dad insisted we go, while they got things ready for my special birthday dinner. They . . . '

Her voice stalled.

'Go on, Eve,' Sam said gently. 'Don't stop now.'

He left the steps and came to sit beside her.

'If we hadn't made the mistake . . . '

He leaned forward.

'What mistake?'

'We mixed up our Saturdays. The market wasn't on until the following week, so we went for a short drive before returning to the Valley. We arrived home in the middle of the afternoon. The lawns had been mown, the table set. It looked beautiful, decorated with Lucy's best china and cutlery. A big, log fire burned in the grate. I can even recall the aroma of lamb roasting in the oven. But there was no sign of Dad or Aunt Lucy.'

'Were they outside?'

Eve linked and unlinked her fingers in her lap. She could feel sweat prickle down her spine. She shook her head.

'I remember the next part as if it were this afternoon.'

'Yes?' he urged.

'I heard sounds coming from upstairs, like whispering.'

'Whispering?'

'I ran up the stairs. I must have been wearing soft-soled shoes. They didn't hear me. Lucy and my father were together in her room. I cried out, and then stood on the landing open-mouthed. I should have stopped my mother from coming up, but somehow I froze to the spot.'

At her side, he put his arms about her shoulders.

'Your mother saw them, too? You poor kid. It must have been awful.'

Eve nodded.

'I should have stopped my mother from coming up. I tell you, I should have stopped her.'

'Hush! You can't blame yourself.'

'If I'd only thought of her!'

'You were seventeen, in shock.'

'You haven't heard the rest of the story.'

He kneeled down beside her, covered her hands with his.

'I'm listening. Don't stop now, Eve.'

'My mother grabbed my hands, dragging me back downstairs. 'Eve,' she cried, 'I didn't want you to know. Lucy has been trying to ruin my marriage for years. You mustn't tell anyone. Swear to me you won't tell anyone.' So I nodded, unable to speak. Then she ran from the house, climbed into her car and drove off. She died half an hour later when the car skidded and ran off the road.'

'And all these years you've kept it locked inside you?'

She brushed his hand aside and sunk deeper into her chair.

'The last thing my mother wanted was a scandal. If I hadn't been there and seen it for myself I'd have thought she was lying to turn me against Lucy, because she knew how much I loved my aunt. But I saw it. I heard their whispers.'

'These things happen in the best of families. Your father and Lucy probably had one of those moments, we all get them, when we're tempted.'

'But Lucy was my mother's sister. I couldn't excuse them,' she cried out. 'Besides, Mother said Lucy had been trying to get Dad for years. I couldn't excuse either of them.'

'I can understand your distress, of course, I can. But I wonder if there wasn't more to it. Did your father talk to you later? Did he try to explain?'

'They both tried, but I couldn't bear to look at them for a while. I wanted nothing to do with them. It troubled me later. I should have given them a hearing, but . . . '

She brushed loose strands of hair back from her face.

'I'll get you a cool drink. We could both do with one.'

He disappeared into the house. Eve began to weep quietly. When Sam returned bearing two tall glasses of mineral water, Eve had her fingers wrapped firmly around the veranda railing. She seemed to have regained some of her composure as she attempted a smile for Sam.

How harshly he'd judged her. Lucy had misled him by describing the problems as a family falling out. He'd never have guessed the tragic events or the aftermath. Yet now he vaguely recalled her mother had been killed in a road accident, and the wave of sympathy it created in the district at the time. People shook their heads and blamed speed and the poor conditions of the road.

'Thanks for telling me, Eve. I know I've put you through the mangle, but you'll feel better later on. I understand so much more about you now. Why, for instance you went overseas when you were so young.'

'I wanted a new life. I'd finished my university degree, I had a sizeable income from my mother's estate, and there was nothing here for me.'

'You couldn't forgive Lucy and your dad?'

'On the few occasions I saw them, I wanted to, but then my heart would turn to steel. I'd remember my mother. After Mum's funeral I asked Dad if he loved Lucy, and he said yes. That's all I needed to know. Mum had been right. I refused to listen to either of them after that.'

Sam knew she wanted to keep talking, and encouraged her.

'It must have been hard cutting yourself off from the only family you knew.'

'I sent Lucy a courtesy note at

Christmas time and on her birthday, but it wouldn't have given her any joy. She kept sending me presents. Once she came to Melbourne and begged me to have lunch with her. It was awful, pretending, hating her for her duplicity, yet remembering how she'd been more a mother to me than my own mother.'

'We're not going to sleep very well tonight. It's still pretty warm. Why don't we stroll down to the dam, toss a few pebbles?'

He took her hand. She didn't protest. He urged her forward, so that they were almost running downhill towards the inky darkness of the water, casting long, thin shadows in front of them. Eve was breathing hard when they dropped to the ground by the water's edge. He watched her pull her knees up to her chin, saw a tear or two glisten in her eyes.

'I shouldn't have come back to Banksia Valley. The memories are too painful. So is the guilt,' she whispered.

'You had to come home to bury the

past. You shouldn't feel guilty. If you'd received our message and arrived back before Lucy died, she could have explained everything. I know she desperately wanted to unburden herself.'

He handed her a pebble.

'Here, see how many skips you can do.'

Eve tired to scud it across the dam, but it hit the water and sank. Ripples orbited from its impact.

'One little stone,' she murmured, as if to herself, 'can make all those waves. One small change in plans started the ripples in my life. I've often thought if the market had been open that day, mother and I might have gone on blissfully ignorant of father's affair with Lucy.'

'By what your mother said, she knew Lucy was trying to steal your father away from her. I think what upset her so much was you finding out.'

'Yes, but she was so distraught. I'm sure she didn't know they were having an affair. I think it was the first time for them. I've been through the what-ifs a hundred times but without getting any answers. And now, with Lucy gone, I'll never learn the full story.'

She sent another stone scudding across the water. In the moonlight he counted.

'One, two, three. You're out of practice, Eve.'

'Once I could beat my dad.'

'Did you see him much afterwards?'

'Once or twice when he was overseas on business, he'd catch up with me. The last time I came home was for his funeral.' Her voice faltered. 'He had a massive heart attack, stress from his job, the doctor said. I thought at the time it had more to do with a guilty conscience. I wanted to forgive him, put it all behind me, but I'd promised my mother.'

'Nobody would have blamed you for breaking that promise.'

'After Dad died, I transferred all my bitterness across to my aunt, instead of trying to heal the wounds. It was immature.'

'But understandable. It's been lonely without your family, hasn't it?'

'I did what I had to and got on with my life.'

She turned to face him. Tears sparkled in her eyes. The urge to kiss her, to comfort her, overcame him. He cupped her chin in his hands, placed his lips to hers. They were soft, surrendering beneath his. He felt a heady desire to deepen the kiss, to let his need for her take control, but the moment wasn't right. He'd be taking advantage of a vulnerable Eve. Gently, he released her, and smiled into her wide eyes.

'Do you feel any better?' he asked quietly.

'Thank you for listening, Sam.'

'Any time. And now we should call it a day.'

He reached for her hands and helped her to her feet. As they walked slowly back up the hill, he asked, 'Have you thought any more about going back to England?'

'Not really. I'm still very uncertain what I want, but I've got three months' leave of absence from my job. I might take some time to reacquaint myself with Melbourne. I'm sure it's vastly different from the city I knew.'

It surprised Sam that she didn't want to get back to Europe, but pleased him, too. With time, they'd get to know one another better. He couldn't deny his physical attraction to her, and suspected he may be falling in love.

'Melbourne's bigger, but it hasn't lost its style, I'm pleased to say. We could visit one of the theatres while you're here.'

'I'd like that.'

They'd reached the veranda. She stood on the step and kissed his cheek.

'Thanks again, Sam,' she said before turning towards the door, but once there she halted.

'You're worried about going into the house, aren't you?' he said.

'It's the whispers. If I heard them again . . .'

He came to her, pushed the door aside, and taking her arm, escorted her into the kitchen.

'You have to forgive them, Eve, or you'll have no peace. They made a mistake, but they loved you. You're sure of that, aren't you?'

'Yes.'

'Concentrate on that. They loved you and you loved them.'

'You're right,' she said, and hurried to her bedroom.

Sam didn't know what else he could say or do. In fact, he wished in a way they hadn't come this far in their relationship. He preferred it when he disliked her. He was in charge then, able to make the decisions which suited his business arrangements. What, he asked himself, was he going to do about Lucy's property now? He needed it for his extensions, and he needed it pronto. He should have been up front with Eve. Tomorrow he would tell her he was the interested buyer . . .

Eve rose early. She slipped into a loose-fitting top and shorts and hurried into the kitchen, hoping to see Sam before he left for Weetangera but he'd already gone. She was disappointed. After last night she felt happier than she had since she'd learned of Lucy's death, thanks to Sam. She had decided to stop thinking about the unanswered questions. Only then could she be sure in her heart that she had forgiven Lucy.

After breakfast, putting on the straw hat, and taking up a small trowel, she strolled out to the front garden to weed the flower beds which skirted the shady veranda. Glancing around, she noted how straw brown and tinder dry the valley looked, after what had obviously been a long, hot summer. She'd seen it like this before, and the bushfires had come.

Nature could be capricious in the bush, having its way. Bushfires raged through this valley the year she was born. Her father often told of how they saved Lucy's house that February and five months later she was born there.

'All the dramas in our lives seem to happen at Banksia Valley,' he had said.

She could see his loving, smiling eyes now as clearly as if he were with her. All the dramas, she thought. He couldn't have known what was to come. She shrugged, determined not to slip back in her thinking. The latest drama? She'd met Sam again. Thinking about him gave her a glow inside.

She kneeled by a bed of pansies, thrust the trowel into the well-mulched earth, lifted the soil and ran her hands through its texture. The only garden she'd known in years were flower boxes in the flats she'd rented.

Absorbed in her thoughts, she didn't hear the car until it began climbing the road to the house. She stood up and, frowning, watched the red sports model curve dangerously fast around the circular drive and settle in a cloud of dust at the front door. Sam's younger brother stepped athletically from the vehicle.

'Hello, there.'

He walked confidently towards her.

'I hope big brother isn't about.'

He still had the winning, lopsided grin she remembered from her golden summers, and instantly warmed to it.

'No, he's up at Weetangera.'

Eve brushed soil from her bare knees, removed the unflattering hat, uncomfortable, as if she were doing something vaguely sneaky. She'd invited Simon to call, but now, remembering Sam's warnings, she hesitated. Sam had called him a manipulator, but to be fair, she had to judge that for herself. She decided to treat him as she would any visitor. He interrupted her thoughts with a mocking laugh.

'Hey, you certainly knocked me over last night. I didn't know big brother had someone living with him. The wily fox. Lovely to see you again, Anne.'

'My name's Eve.'

Annoyed, she almost didn't accept

his hand, and when he squeezed her fingers in an uncomfortably familiar way, she wished she hadn't. As she stared into what she now decided were bold blue eyes, Sam's warning flashed into her mind.

'You're mistaken. We're not living together. Through a set of unforeseen and embarrassing circumstances, we happen to be occupying the same house,' she said coldly.

Unperturbed, he appraised her.

'Well, I wouldn't trust old Sam. Take it from me, he's a fast worker that brother of mine and you're a desirable lady. I can't believe you're the one we used to call Freckles. The sun on your hair makes it look like shot silk and the blue of your eyes is something else.'

He was really laying it on, but the handsome Simon's well-practised art of wooing women failed to impress her. Her lips tight, she gazed back at him. He broke into a warm laugh.

'Ah, yes, I can see now why we called you Freckles.'

His finger reached towards her cheek, but she swept it aside in a rush of irritation. Again he laughed.

'You still have one or two, and very attractive they are.'

'Do you mind?' She stepped away. 'I think you should leave.'

'Sorry if I've stepped out of line. You can blame it on my big brother. He taught me everything I know about women.'

'Oh, come on, Simon.'

'So he's hoodwinked you, too. He's living in the same house with you, isn't he? And I'm willing to wager he's . . . well . . . you know what.'

Crimson-faced, she drew herself to her full height and glared at him.

'Just one minute. There are things you need to understand.'

If he thought she could be influenced by smart talk and insincere compliments, or his references to Sam, he was wrong.

'You'd better come inside. I know I need a cool drink.'

Resting her trowel and hat on the window sill, she led the way into the house, aware that he followed closely behind.

'This isn't what it seems,' she began, her annoyance somewhat abated by the time they were seated with glasses of iced water in hand.

'The sooner you understand there is absolutely nothing going on between me and your brother, the better.'

'You don't have to explain away anything to me.'

'Of course I don't, but I choose to. I arrived from England for my aunt's funeral to find Sam had moved in here, with my aunt's permission, while your property is being renovated. Since I'm not going to be here very long, there was no point in asking him to move out.'

Simon nodded.

'So he twisted your arm?'

'No, he didn't. I invited him to stay.'

'You realise what you've done? You

might lose the place.'

'What place?'

'This one. He got rid of me from the family business.'

'He told me you moved to the city.'

His golden-boy looks deserted him when he sniggered.

'I suppose that's how he'd explain my absence. The truth is, once my father signed everything over to the family strong man, he turfed me out.'

'Surely not. I can't believe Sam would be so heartless.'

Though she protested, her thoughts clouded with doubts as she remembered his earlier uncompromising attitude to her. Simon's mouth widened. He was laughing bitterly.

'So he's got to you, too. But there's no mistake, Princess, I've been cut off. I get a third-world monthly allowance, nothing more. His gods are money, success and women in that order. Women, he loves and leaves when he's used them up.'

'Will you stop assuming your brother

131

and I are having an affair?' she snapped. 'Please.'

Deep in her heart she felt profound disappointment. Did she really know Sam? She changed the subject.

'You look pretty prosperous. Obviously despite Sam you've been successful. Are you in legal practice?'

'No. Too dull. I pulled out of university. I helped my father on the property for some time and then went into marketing. At the moment I'm setting up my own real estate chain in this area. Land and houses up here are at a premium. It's trendy to have a few acres, clean air and a horse. Prices have skyrocketed.'

'Really?'

'Business people are paying the earth for hobby farms within commuting distance of the city and the airport. There's enormous potential for this sleepy, little township. I'm buying up as much acreage as I can and subdividing into small farmlets. In a few years, Eve, you won't know it. There'll be a supermarket, a restaurant, the lot.'

Enthusiasm glinted in his eyes, his smile. His keenness impressed her, yet imagining the farms and orchards cut up and the intimate township developed into a busy supermarket to service the new settlers troubled her.

'Won't the whole character and charm of the place disappear?'

'It's called progress, Eve.'

Was that what she wanted to happen to this beautiful bushland tract? She tried to arrest her negative feelings. She tried telling herself that after she returned to England, she doubted if she'd ever see Australia again. So why would she care? No family, no Banksia Valley. What was left to come home to? She felt a tug on her heartstrings, an emptiness in her stomach.

'This sounds like the ideal time to get into the real estate game. I had no idea the land out here was in such demand,' she commented, hoping he wouldn't notice the flatness of her voice.

'It's ripe for the picking. Given the right marketing plan I can see boom years ahead, dollars in the till. And I'm looking for a partner.'

'Have you tried your brother?'

'A waste of time. Sam wouldn't lend me the money. Besides he's poured the family fortune into that ridiculous tourist dream of his, going against the trend, extending the vineyard instead of dividing it into small lots and selling up. He's practically broke himself.'

'Can't you appeal to your father?'

'Sam controls the money. I don't suppose you'd be interested.'

He stood up, waved a hand dismissively.

'Of course, you wouldn't.'

'Wouldn't what? Let you sell this place for me? I might.'

'You're joking, Princess.'

'About what?'

'You mean you don't know?'

He stared at her.

'Don't know what?'

'Your aunt promised this place to

134

Sam. He needs the land to further his plans for the vineyard and tourist bit. Now don't tell me the cunning rat didn't mention it.'

8

Slowly, deliberately, Eve stood up, trying to take in Simon's statement, trying not to give way to anger and disappointment. She had to absorb fully and consider his words.

As she rinsed the glasses under the tap, her back to her visitor, it all became clear to her. Sam wanted Banksia Valley and her aunt had agreed. It answered so many questions — why he had been upset at her unexpected return, his dislike of her, his public attachment to her aunt, his annoyance at her hesitation in making a decision to return to England, his warning last evening to stay away from Simon.

He'd ingratiated himself with her aunt, persuaded her to sell, probably at below market-value price, but his plans went awry when Lucy died before the sale went through. And then Eve turned up unexpectedly on the doorstep. After their bad start, he'd resorted to pretending a romantic interest in her, just to win her over. Sam Easton was a fake!

She fought back anger and tears. What she had to say would be addressed directly to Sam. It had nothing to do with Simon and no good could come of involving him. Taking up a dish cloth, she began drying the glasses, busying her trembling fingers at the sink.

'He mentioned a buyer, but at the time I'd just heard about my aunt and wasn't thinking too clearly. Anyway that doesn't alter anything,' she said slowly. 'If you call back in a few days' time, we can talk about the sale details.'

Her voice cracked, her eyes misted. She damned Sam Easton, but she hung on to her pride. Simon mustn't know how much his revelation had hurt. As she placed the clean glasses on the shelf, hidden from his vision, she fingered away the tears of betrayal and composed herself.

'That's generous of you, Princess, but you'll have a fight on your hands from Sam, all the way to the auction.'

'Then we won't have an auction. I'll sell privately. You can arrange that, can't you? Keep it quiet?'

Sam wasn't going to get Banksia Valley at any price. A watery smile tugged at the corners of her mouth. Sam would pay plenty for his duplicity, and not in money.

'Sure I can, but big brother will go crazy.'

'I can cope with that.'

'Them's fighting words, little lady. A kiss to seal our agreement?'

By her side, with practised ease he turned her face to his and covered her mouth. She stiffened. She hated Simon's glibness, his assumption that he was every woman's fantasy. She hated the Easton brothers. What more was there to say? He smiled down on her as she wrestled from his hold.

'I'm too late, aren't I? Old Sam's

already staked his claim on you. But I warn you, Princess, he's not the marrying kind, if that's what you're after.'

'I'm not,' she snapped.

'Whatever you say. I'll give you a call with a firm estimate of the property's value and then we'll list it. Of course, you realise we'd get a better price if we subdivided. But it's your call. Thanks again. You're a good sport.'

Simon had called her a good sport many times during her golden summers. Today it sounded forced, insincere. Already uneasiness stirred with her. In truth she didn't trust Simon, or his older brother.

Outside, the sun had disappeared. The sky looked dark and threatening. The freshening north wind lashed at her hair.

'We need rain,' Simon commented as they walked to his car.

But Eve only nodded, her focus on just one thing — to find Sam and confront him.

As he swung into the car, Simon suggested, 'There's no need for Sam to know about our arrangement, is there? Tell him you've engaged a real estate agent. You know we're looking at six figures.'

She sucked in hot air.

'That much? I had no idea.'

And Sam hadn't bothered to mention it, she thought cynically.

'Don't worry, I can be pretty shrewd myself when it comes to business,' she added.

Simon grinned as he engaged the engine and the sleek machine moved off. Eve shaded her eyes with her hand as she watched the progress down the driveway and out on to the road. Then her gaze moved to the well-defined walking track leading to Weetangera. Instinctively, she wanted to storm up it to find her quarry, but she resisted, taking the time to change into solid walking shoes. Next she retrieved the straw hat from the sill where she'd left it, and began her journey with long, purposeful strides.

Sam Easton thought he'd been clever, but he'd lose out. He wouldn't get Banksia Valley, even if she had to fight him in every court in the land, even if it took every bit of her savings, even if she had to stay in Australia and live in the house for the rest of her life. At that point, she shivered.

As she hoped, she found Sam in the giant, iron building. He was talking with another man, a plan spread on a workbench before them. She coughed to announce herself.

'Eve, what a pleasant surprise,' he said.

A wide smile accompanied the greeting, a smile which she was about to turn to a curl of the lips.

'This is my site manager, Gary Winters. Gary, Eve Sutherland. She owns Banksia Valley, he added, where-upon Winters offered his hand. Eve smiled.

'It's a nice property,' he said.

'Yes. There's a lot of interest in

buying it,' she commented, directing her attention to Sam.

'Thanks, Gary, I'll catch you later,' Sam said quickly, folding up the plans as if anxious to get rid of his manager.

Sam came to her side, reached for her hand.

'Did you sleep well?'

She stepped away.

'Do you really care?'

'I detect some acid in your voice.'

'I had a visitor this morning.'

'Good. You need some company right now.'

'Your brother.'

Sam's face clouded.

'Simon? And what did he have to say for himself?'

'That you're the person who made Lucy the good offer to buy the Valley.

'I made it on behalf of Hillside Holdings, my company.'

'So why didn't you tell me?'

'I'm a shareholder and chairman of directors. What difference does it make?

value, like any other buyer.'

'It makes a difference to me. You withheld from me the information that you were the buyer. Why didn't you come out and say you were the person who cared about the land and whom Lucy trusted?'

'Because in your frame of mind, you wouldn't have agreed. Anyway, I don't believe you gave me the chance to explain.'

'Nonsense, you've had ample opportunity since then.'

She pushed back tendrils of her hair which had escaped the straw hat and gave a hollow laugh.

'What a gullible fool you must think me. You wheedled your way into my aunt's good books all those months. It was so damned obvious, staring me in the face, yet I didn't pick up, because I credited you with some integrity when it came to Lucy's affairs. I thought you genuinely admired her.'

'Calm down, Eve. You're blowing this

right out of proportion.'

'I haven't finished yet. You wanted control of Lucy's property and were prepared to lie and cheat to get it. How you must have laughed and schemed behind my back the last days. Were you ever going to tell me?'

Eve didn't pause for an answer.

'Well, Sam Easton, I've got news for you. You've wasted your time, because I asked Simon to sell the property for me. Your bid will be refused.'

'Eve, I can understand your surprise, but be very careful in dealing with Simon. He is not to be trusted.'

She laughed harshly.

'And you are?' she said in a tone full of derision.

'I didn't intend to deceive you. Because we got off to a bad start, thanks to me running off at the mouth about you not caring about Lucy, I decided you wouldn't be receptive to anything I proposed. So I delayed telling you. I was waiting for the right moment. You're not going to believe this, but last night I decided I'd tell you today.'

'How very convenient.'

'Answer me this. Would you have agreed to the sale if I'd told you I was the buyer the day after you arrived?'

She hesitated.

'I'd have considered it, if you'd been honest with me, but to pretend all that stuff about Lucy . . . '

'You can't honestly believe I'm that devious. I admired your aunt very much. She was highly intelligent, amusing, perceptive and placid, unlike someone I could name. She'd have picked me for a phoney immediately. The fact is she was grateful to have someone around who genuinely cared for her,' he said wryly.

Her anger eased. She wanted to believe him, but could she trust him?

'I don't want you inside my house again,' she retorted, titling her chin, denying the doubts which crowed in on her. 'You'll find your bags packed and waiting for you on the veranda when you're ready to call and pick them up. Don't bother to knock, I won't be in.'

She turned away.

'Suit yourself. When you've cooled down, you'll realise your aunt wanted me to have the property. She knew I wouldn't make a killing by selling it off to developers, which is exactly what Simon will do. He'll buy it from you and then sub-divide.'

'He hasn't got any money.'

'He'll con a loan from someone. He's good at that. Look, Eve, I wasn't making it up when I said I discussed how I intended to use the land with your aunt, and she liked the idea.'

'Well, of course she did. You call Simon a con. You could talk your way into Buckingham Palace with a gun strapped to your waist.'

She wheeled around, the light of battle flickering in her eyes.

'Does it really matter who buys the place as long as you can rush back to England?' he drawled with infuriating calm.

'It matters.'

Why, she asked herself, as she stormed out of the shed and back to the bush track. There, more questions ambushed her. Why would a man with Sam's impeccable background and reputation as a lawyer set out to beguile a sick, defenceless woman into selling him her land? Yes, he'd deliberately withheld the information that he wanted to buy the Valley, but sooner or later she'd have found out, and it was Simon who'd hinted that Sam wouldn't pay the market price. Sam mentioned the Easton family finances had suffered some kind of major loss. Maybe that drove him to act out of character.

Breathing quickly, Eve slipped through the gate between the properties and began the steep descent down to Lucy's house, Lucy's property. She repeated the words, Lucy's property, over in her head several times. Of course it was Lucy's place. It could never be hers, not after the events of her seventeenth birthday, not after losing the opportunity to reconcile with the aunt who had once been closer to her than her mother.

She glanced over the parched land beyond the homestead, filtered by towering eucalyptus, thirst, shedding their leaves like confetti in the wind, the dam beyond, it's waterline slowly diminishing. She shivered in the heat, aware that the continuing dryness spelled danger, but aware, too, that in time the land would reawaken to autumn's cooling winds and gentle rains.

And in her solitude, it came to her that Lucy would hate her beloved land divided up into small hobby farms. Sam knew that. He'd tried to convince her, but because he'd deceived her, played with her emotions, hurt her, she'd refused to listen. But Sam was the rightful inheritor of the Valley. He loved the land. Lucy had planned it that way, but death had intervened.

Foolishly, she'd allowed Simon to influence her when her instinct told her he had a secret agenda. When Sam arrived to pick up his things she'd tell him the property was his. She would return to Europe. With nothing to draw her back to Australia, she could restart her life. If only she'd thought things through before storming up to Weetangera earlier.

In her heart, she'd known from day one of her arrival home that the property belonged to Sam. He was at home here. She was not.

Sam arrived wearing a black T-shirt, damp with sweat. Faded, cut-down jeans clung tightly to his body. His dark hair was in disarray, and a day's stubble shadowed his dark complexion. He stood at the door, grim-faced, when she answered the knock. Her heart missed a beat.

'Sorry to disturb you. I came for my things. You said you'd leave them on the veranda, but I don't see them anywhere.'

'You'd better come in. I have something to say.'

'Haven't you said enough already?'

'This is the most important.'

Turning, she walked into the house, relieved to hear his footsteps behind her. She imagined the scowl he must have on his face.

'You look as if you could do with a cool drink,' she said when they reached the kitchen.

'Forget the niceties. What's this all about?'

'You'd better sit down.'

'No thanks.'

'Please yourself, but I need a drink.'

She poured two glasses of juice, slid one across the table in his direction, and plopped into a chair. He remained standing in the doorway, watching her, his mouth drawn into a tight line.

'You can have Banksia Valley. You can draw up the necessary documents for me to sign as soon as you like.'

He looked at her sharply, ran a hand through his hair.

'I think I'd better sit down after all. This isn't some kind of sick joke?'

He took the chair opposite her.

'I've never been more serious.'

'What changed your mind?'

'Lucy.'

He frowned.

'I don't follow.'

'I was coming back from Weetangera when I realised that this place belongs to you. It was almost as though Lucy were speaking to me, telling me you cared for it and she wanted you to have it. Do you believe in that kind of thing?'

'Not really, but I'm glad you do.'

He grinned.

'She knew the golden summers here ended on my seventeenth birthday, and I'd sell quickly just to be rid of the place. The last thing she wanted was to have it sub-divided. You'd never have agreed to that. I almost did by giving Simon the sale contract.'

'I think Lucy did speak to you.'

He smiled, captivating her.

'Her worst fear was that her Eden would be broken up and auctioned off to the highest bidders. I assured her I wouldn't let that happen, but unfortunately we didn't get around to legalising my purchase.'

'If only you hadn't deceived me. I hated that, Sam.'

'I'm very sorry, Eve. I thought I was being honest, not devious, by waiting for the right moment. If Simon hadn't come along . . . '

'You can't blame him. He's trying to establish a real estate business, having been cut off from the family fortune.'

'There is no family fortune, Eve. Simon gambled most of it away. The only assets he couldn't get his hands on were the house and the vineyards, because my mother persuaded father to put them into my name when she discovered Dad had given Simon every penny of their ready money.'

Eve gasped.

'How awful. You hinted at something once or twice, but I didn't think! If only I'd had some inkling. I ignored most of what he said, but when he told me you wanted the land, well, I lost my cool.

He really got stuck into you. He blames you for his situation.'

'He blames everyone but himself. He didn't try to come on to you, did he? I'll wring his miserable neck if he did.'

'No,' she lied quietly. 'He seemed convinced that you and I are an item.'

She smiled, amused at the very idea.

'And are we?'

The fire in his eyes flickered to a warm glow. He looked at her with a gentleness she had never imagined possible, and her heart leaped. Suppose there was a chance for them. But, no! That could never be!

'You take the joke too far,' she said in an attempt at a light-hearted reply. 'But I'm really sorry about you and Simon. Your dad must be devastated.'

'I'm pleased to say he's recovering well from the stroke. So now you know about my family skeleton. It seems we all have them closeted away some-where.'

'It seems that way.'

'But it's getting easier for you, surely?'

She shook her head.

'Talking about it was a positive step, and I'm grateful to you for listening, but putting the past behind me will take a long time. I fled from the truth, put my hands over my eyes and ears and wished it away, when I should have confronted it. No wonder I find it hard to trust people. That's why I was so ready to doubt you. I thought you were a hard, rude, money-hungry brute.'

She laughed.

'And I thought you were a snobbish, cold-hearted, money-grabbing . . . Damn it all, I've run out of adjectives,' he exclaimed.

'It's just as well.'

They both laughed.

'Eve, now you trust me, am I pushing too hard if I get a valuer out here tomorrow to explain to you what the property's worth?'

His dark glance caught hers. She

flipped tendrils of hair back from her cheek.

'There's no need to get a valuer. I'm not selling it to you.'

He threw up his hands.

'Damn it, you've just finished saying . . . '

Her voice tinkled with laughter.

'You thanked me for trusting you. How about you trusting me? I'm not selling you the property. It's a gift.'

'I won't take it.'

He folded his arms across his chest, shook his head.

'No way.'

'I can't gift wrap it, but if I could the card would read, *To Sam with love from Lucy. Thank you for everything you've done for me.* I can see her smiling, wherever she might be now. She'd be proud of me.'

'I think I need that drink after all,' he said, picking up the glass of juice and downing it in two quick gulps.

He ran his tongue along his moist lips. His action drew Eve's glance. She coloured and stood up.

'So, when can you have the papers drawn up?'

'Honestly, it's a lovely thought, but I can't accept. Take some time to think about it. An idea which might appeal is for you to accept shares in Hillside Holdings to the property's value.'

She shook her head.

'No, Sam. Banksia Valley is yours, no strings attached. I've decided to go back to England.'

He reached out to her, took her hand in his.

'I wish you wouldn't. Stay a bit longer, give yourself some time to get to know the place again, to get to know me better.'

9

Sam didn't want to lose Eve. He knew that now. He'd only just found her.

He felt a knot in his stomach. True love had finally caught up with him.

Eve looked at him, hesitation in her beautiful eyes.

'Stay a little longer, Eve,' he whispered, tilting her chin in his hand, kissing her.

They were the softest, sweetest lips he had tasted as she surrendered to him, but the moment passed in a flash. She touched his face, ran her fingers down his neck, as she eased away.

'I can't stay, Sam. I have to put the past behind me. I'm doing that slowly, but living here makes it doubly hard. For me this house is jinxed.'

She spread her hands in front of her as if asking him to understand. He sighed.

'We could find a place nearby for you to rent.'

'Would that really make any difference? You'd still be living in the house. I'd be in and out of here, reminded again and again of something I desperately want to forget.'

'You can't run away from the past again, Eve.'

'I wouldn't be running away. I see it as a fresh start.'

'So you've already made plans to leave?'

'I'll do that tomorrow. I'll get the earliest flight back. We'll have a few more days together at most.'

'I'll miss you.'

In the time she'd been here, she'd worked her way into his heart. He loved to see her blush, to watch her tuck her hair behind one ear, tilt her chin, little mannerisms which told him of the vulnerability and softness which lay beneath her plucky surface. She smiled and laughed at the things he enjoyed. They'd shared their bad experiences and understood. And now she planned to disappear from his life as suddenly as she had reappeared. He couldn't let that happen.

'By the way, Sam,' her voice arrested his thoughts, 'you have forgotten, I hope, that this morning I asked you to move out. I couldn't remain in the house at night unless you were around.'

He laughed.

'I suspected that might be the case. You must have been really ticked off with me when you told me to pack my bags.'

'I was disillusioned.'

She took a mild swipe at him. He dodged her blow with ease.

'And how about now?'

'I think you're fishing for compliments. All I'm saying is I've withdrawn my ultimatum.'

While they shared the house, he'd have time and the opportunity to talk her out of leaving. She had two, perhaps three days. Then in a moment of raw honesty, he told himself to get real. This wasn't some business deal to be won by negotiating with a will of iron and a pack of the right cards. He didn't hold the aces, and his future happiness was at stake. He'd have to handle this delicate affair of the heart with sincerity and understanding.

He sensed Eve was drawn to him. He'd seen it, felt it in her responses to him. If he could make her forget the past. He'd woo her, help her to understand how magnificent their lives together could be, starting with tonight.

'Good, because from tonight I'm going to be around you as much as possible. Let's enjoy our time together. Shall we dine out again, go dancing?'

'It's a nice idea, but it's so hot.'

She drew loose tendrils of hair back from her face. It was beautiful hair, long, lustrous, made for male hands to caress. The idea of staying home had much more appeal than dinner and dancing.

'Shall I order a takeaway?' he asked.

'Let me prepare a chicken salad and

we can eat out on the veranda, listen to some music, which reminds me, you used to play the guitar, didn't you?'

'I strummed a few notes. Still do when I get the urge. The guitar's in my room.'

'Could you get the urge tonight?'

'Tonight I could get the urge to do anything for you.'

'Don't overdo the generosity. I might ask the impossible.'

'Such as?'

He waited. There was no impossible.

'That you accept my gift of the property.'

She hurried off then, denying him the chance to answer.

Turning at the door, she added, 'While I'm preparing dinner, you'll have time to shower. Oh, and bring out your guitar.'

The air had cooled slightly as Sam opened a chilled bottle of wine after dinner, and poured two glasses.

'You haven't told me much about your plans,' Eve said. 'When will everything be ready to open to the public? Who's going to run the accommodation side of things?'

'It'll take around three months to complete the renovations, and I plan to run it myself. I want to make it a real showpiece, get on to the overseas visitors' itinerary listings. It's a dream I've had for years. I'll remain a silent partner in the law firm, only take special clients. As you know, I'm a bush boy at heart, always have been.'

He moved his chair back from the table, folded his arms across his chest and gave a long sigh.

'What do you intend for Lucy's valley, your valley?' she asked.

He leaned back in his chair.

'The meal was delicious by the way. Thanks.'

'Your turn tomorrow night.' She tilted her head. 'Now, about the Valley.'

'On the drawing-board, I've turned the house into tourist accommodation, adding en suites and little kitchenettes. Would it worry you to lose the bedroom you seem to love?'

'I did love it, but not any more. Haven't you guessed how uncomfortable this house makes me? I spend as much time as I can outdoors.'

'I thought it was the heat. So you're sure you won't mind losing your room?'

'None. Do whatever it takes.'

'Lucy and I had a great time planning the gardens around the house. They won't be substantially altered. We'll set up picnic barbecue areas, and encourage some wild life in, maybe kangaroos, wombats, ducks on the dam, which will be known as a pond, of course.'

He laughed.

'Lucy and I agreed it sounds better. As for the acres beyond — the big players began eyeing our comparatively small family holding once we mortgaged it. So we need to develop our enterprise or we risk a take-over. The pasture will become vineyards. Do you approve?'

'It's yours, Sam, to do as you wish.

The main thing is, Lucy liked your ideas.'

'Some of them were hers, but I'd value your opinion. How do you really feel about the house being gutted and its character being changed?'

'OK. As I said earlier, the place has lost the charm it once had for me.'

'But later, when you feel better about Lucy, you might regret it.'

'I don't think so. Sam, why don't you play something on the guitar?'

'Sure.'

He took up the instrument which rested against the wall of the house, and seated himself on the steps of the veranda.

'I should warn you, I'm a bit rusty.'

He plucked a few strings, tuned up the instrument, and then began to play. His choice of music caught at Eve's breath, it was so romantic. She picked up on the tune, and hummed quietly in the half light. The title of the song began to take on special meaning as Sam sang the verses of 'You Were

Always On My Mind.'

When the final notes sounded, he said. 'Come and sit beside me, Eve. Do you realise how often you've been on my mind?'

'Please, Sam, don't make it any harder for me than it is. I can't stay.'

Her eyes ached with the tears she mustn't shed, her voice stammered over the words she had to say.

'We deserve a chance,' he said. 'We could make it. I've fallen in love with you, Eve. I think you know that.'

She hadn't known, but deep within her had lain a hope, and that hope sprang into reality with his words. He loved her! Eve longed to feel his arms around her, to be protected, to share her life with him. She longed to reach out and pluck and hold to her heart for ever this chance at happiness. Sam was the only man she'd loved.

'I didn't know, Sam,' she murmured.

'I think you love me, too.'

'This is happening too fast.'

'It has to. You've only given me

twenty-four hours or so to convince you to stay.'

'And if I do stay? What then?'

He came to her, kneeling at the side of her chair, clasping her hand.

'Eve, will you marry me?'

She looked down at him, her heart in turmoil. Sam, the Valley, both were inextricably caught up in her past. If they could walk away from here together, but it was too much to ask of Sam, who was at one with his environment. For them to have a relationship to last for ever and a day, she had to resolve in her mind the problems which made this place both alien and beckoning at the one time.

'Sam, I love you. I think I have since I was ten.'

She smiled down at him, ran her hand through his unruly hair.

'And I can't believe you've asked me to marry you. It's a dream come true. I want to be your wife, but I couldn't live here, feeling the way I do about the Valley. And I won't go into this relationship while I'm carrying so much baggage from the past. It would be a bad beginning.'

He stood up and reached out to her, urged her from the chair and took her in his arms, whispering against her hair.

'I could make all the ugliness disappear. I love you, Eve. My love is strong enough for both of us.'

'It's best if I return to Europe for a few months, give myself time away from this house to think things through. And you'll have time to finish your project and get it up and running. I'll come back in the spring, and if we still feel the same, we'll be married.'

'If I let you go, you mightn't come back.'

His hand caressed the length of her hair, his breath feathered across her heated cheeks.

'It's a risk I don't want to take.'

'I will. How could I not come back to the man I love with all my heart?'

She traced the soft pad of her finger

over his strong features, drew his gaze to hers.

'I'll come back, I promise.'

'I trust you, Eve. I know you will.'

He held her at arms' length, light shining in his dark eyes.

'I've thought of a wonderful idea. We'll build a new chalet for the tourists, and I'll have the house renovated for us. We'll live here. Hey, Lucy,' he said and looked skyward, 'are you listening? Eve and I will live here. We could even have the wedding ceremony here.'

Eve wrenched herself free of him.

'Please, Sam, I could never live in this house. Every time I go inside I tense up. If you hadn't been staying here I wouldn't have lasted more than the first night.'

'But we'll renovate. All you have to do is tell me what changes to make.'

She smiled briefly at his enthusiasm.

'You'd have to pull the whole place down. At night I lie awake re-running everything, thinking, wondering what made Lucy and my father cheat on my mother. I don't hear the whispers any more, thank goodness. That must mean I'm making some progress, but it's slow. If only I knew the truth.'

'Come back here where you belong.'

She returned to his arms and nestled her head into his well-muscled chest.

'I'm being paranoid, but it's how I feel.'

'You're being honest. If you need six months, take it. It's a short time compared to the rest of our lives. I know in the end you won't let the past beat you.'

'Thank you,' she said, a tear in her voice, 'for being here for me.'

He tilted her chin, kissed her gently.

'Where else would I be? Will you sleep tonight? I could stay downstairs if it makes you more comfortable.'

'I'll be fine. Having you too close might not be such a good idea. We could be tempted. Now, Sam, if you've got work to do, don't be afraid to say so. I think I'll stay out here for a bit. It's still very hot inside.'

He planted a kiss on her forehead.

'Call me if you want an escort inside. And by the way, I'll be at the office in the morning arranging the transfer of papers for Banksia Valley and then I'll go on to Weetangera. Why don't you bring a picnic lunch up there?'

She caught up his hand, put it to her lips.

'I can't believe you love me.'

'You just want me to say it again.'

She nodded.

'Good-night, my dearest love.'

Eve listened to his firm footsteps as they trod down the hallway. Even they had strength and confidence. She had found her man, and after she untangled her emotions, she would have him. As she sat down in her chair, her eyelids grew heavy. It had been an extraordinary day.

Her last thoughts before she drifted into sleep were of Lucy. If only she'd heard Lucy and her father out, listened to their side of the story . . .

10

It was after eleven next morning, a menacing grey day. The heat had sucked all the air from the house. In a lather of perspiration, Eve took a cool drink on to the veranda after packing some of her clothes, and making phone arrangements to fly out the day after tomorrow.

The smell of smoke gusted in on the hot wind. A bushfire was burning away beyond the Valley, the radio news bulletin said, but fresh outbreaks were expected as the scorching heat continued to dry out the land. The sound of dogs barking at Weetangera carried to her on the shrill north wind, as did the engine of a motor scooter up her driveway. She hurried to join the mailwoman, who slowed long enough to thrust letters into her hand and shout, 'You're popular today. Can't hang around. I have to get the deliveries done before I pass out in this heat.'

'Thanks.'

Eve grasped the letters tightly lest the wind wrench them from her. Bills, she thought. Gripping her straw hat with her free hand, she tossed them on to the table to open later, but the handwriting leaped out at her. Her breath caught in her throat.

Twice readdressed, this last time to Banksia Valley, Lucy's letters had finally found her! In death, her aunt would at last speak to her.

Did she really want to open them, though, now that she had decided on her future and felt comfortable about it? These letters might induce another wave of uncertainty. But she'd refused to listen to Lucy once, and second chances didn't come all that often.

Dropping into a chair she sorted through them with trembling fingers. There were four in all. She arranged them in post-dated order. Then, her heart on hold, she released the flap of the first letter.

It was just as Sam had told her. Lucy wrote that she was seriously ill, begging Eve to come home so that she could talk. It ended, *I love you, Eve. I always have, and I'm desperately sorry you found out about your father and me in the way that you did. It was the very last thing we wanted to happen. Please forgive me.*

Eve took a gulp of her drink. Her hands continued to shake, her heart to beat as if time had almost run out, as she opened the next letter. It, like the first, said much the same, as did the third. If only she'd received them, she'd have come back in a flash, talked to Lucy, held her hand through her illness, and told her she loved her, too. But, alas, nothing her aunt said helped her to understand why Lucy and her father had betrayed her mother. How could there be an excuse for that?

A knot developed in the pit of her stomach. She jammed the open letters into the pocket of her shorts. The fourth one sat unopened on the table beside her drink. It looked thicker, the writing less certain. Did it tell her anything new? She picked up Lucy's last letter. Slipping her index finger under the flap, she loosened the seal, and on the edge of her chair, removed four pages.

Dearest Eve, it began, *I wanted to explain to you in person, but I've given up hope of seeing you now. I don't blame you for not coming. You reacted as any young protected girl would when you found your father and me together. But, for your father's sake, I cannot die peacefully until you know the truth.*

Eve's eyes grew misty as she read on. Through a haze she finished the first page. By the time she reached the fourth, her tears fell unabated. The ink on the page ran as she wept. Dabbing the paper with a tissue, she shuffled the pages, reading them again and again, until spent, she fell back into her chair and took several deep breaths, allowing her mind to absorb what she had read.

Minutes later, she still sat there. The breeze tugged at the letter which lay in her lap. She grabbed at it and folded it back into its envelope. What on earth am I doing here, she asked herself. Jumping to her feet, she ran down the steps, along the path to the track leading to Weetangera and up the steep incline. Twigs and dry grass spiked and scratched her feet through her sandals, the howling wind impeded her progress, but nothing deterred her.

By the time she reached the iron shed, she was shouting Sam's name. He looked up when he saw her in the doorway, smiled, hurried to her side.

'You brought lunch? Lovely. Hey, no hat, and you can hardly breathe. What's the matter, Eve?'

'Nothing,' she shrilled, 'except for Lucy's letters. They've been re-addressed here!'

She brandished the last one in her hand.

'I understand everything now.'

'And you're not halfway excited, sweetheart. Great news.'

He put his arm about her.

'Here, read it.'

She pushed the letter towards him.

'Read it, Sam.'

'Let's find a shady tree somewhere. I'll get one of the blokes to make us a flask of tea, and then I want you to tell me what's in the letter. I won't read it because it's personal between you and your aunt.'

Eve reached up and brushed his hair back from his forehead.

'I don't think I realised before how thoughtful you are, not like me. I sound off first and think later. But this is something to sound off about.'

She found it hard to control the pitch of her voice.

Using a painter's plank across two drums, someone had made a temporary seat in the shade of several trees. Sam sat her there and went in search of a vacuum flask of tea. He returned only minutes later and poured a cup and handed it to Eve.

'Over to you,' he said, 'but take your time.'

She cleared her throat, overcome by the enormity of what she had discovered, and launched with a breathless rush, into her story.

'It's amazing, unbelievable. Did you know Lucy and my mother were twins?'

He nodded. 'Lucy told me.'

'They both fell in love with my father, but he asked Lucy to marry him. One night, he and Lucy had a tiff because Dad was tired of them going out as a threesome, and insisted they leave Mum behind. Lucy didn't agree so Dad went off on his own, had too much to drink, and returned to the house late at night to apologise. He met Mum, probably on the veranda and they made love. Lucy didn't say so, but my guess is Mum took advantage of Dad having too much to drink. Mother was very beautiful. I often wondered how she could have had such a plain child!'

Eve twisted and untwisted the envelope in her hand. Looking up, she met Sam's incredulous gaze.

'Plain? You were never plain, even with pigtails.'

'You have such wonderful eyes, Sam. They wouldn't see plainness.'

She kissed him lightly on the cheek.

'So your father did the honourable thing, married your mother and broke Lucy's heart.'

'Not exactly. My mother soon discovered she was pregnant.'

'Well, well. With you, Eve?'

'Yes. So all those years my father lived in a second-rate marriage because of me, but not once did he allow me to glimpse his unhappiness. And I returned his love by doubting him and his integrity.'

Her flow of words dried up.

'And what of Lucy? You didn't guess she loved your dad?'

Eve tried again, straining to speak.

'No. The amazing thing is, after my mother found out she was pregnant, the three of them made a pact. They decided Mum and Dad would marry for the sake of the baby and on my seventeenth birthday, after dinner, Mother would tell me she was divorcing Dad, so he could marry his true love, Lucy. They thought I'd be old enough to cope by then.'

She turned anxious eyes on Sam.

'But the plan went a bit haywire,' he said tenderly.

'Lucy blamed herself. She and Dad kept their part of the bargain, but on that day they were alone in the house. Father was upstairs changing when she went to ask him something and somehow they didn't think they were doing anything wrong.'

'Can you understand that, Eve?'

She nodded.

'Of course, I can. How they kept their feelings under wraps for so many years, I don't know. I wondered why Dad only visited the Valley on special occasions. He was always too busy to come when Mother dropped me off at

Lucy's for holidays and when she accompanied him on country and overseas business trips. Everything makes sense now.'

Eve handed the empty mug back to Sam.

'What's surprising is why your mother stormed out that day when she already knew about Lucy and your father, and was preparing to tell you that night.'

'Lucy thought Mother probably still hoped it wouldn't happen. But when I saw them together, she realised the truth had to come out. Her marriage was over. She couldn't handle it because she didn't have Lucy's strength. In a way I feel sorry for Mum. She must have loved Dad a lot.'

'It was a selfish love, Eve, a destructive, one-way love. She took advantage of Lucy and ruined her chance of marriage and children.'

As he poured himself a mug of tea, Eve thought again of the after-math of that long-ago birthday, and knew he was right.

'Mum asked me to swear I'd never tell anyone what I'd seen. She was afraid of the scandal. It's ironic, isn't it? If she hadn't turned the car over and died, Lucy and Dad would have had many happy years together. As it was, they blamed each other and themselves for her death, and hardly met again after that day. In death, my mother achieved what she couldn't have hoped for in life. She succeeded in keeping them apart.'

Sam put down his mug, opened his arms to her.

'And she cost you, too, sweetheart. Cry, Eve. Let it all out. It's over.'

'I don't want to cry. I've done that,' she said, feeling the power and strength of being close to him. 'I'm a little numb, but there's joy in my heart, too. Lucy's letter has released me. I can feel the freedom of loving her and Dad again as I haven't done in years.'

He cupped her chin with his hand.

'You will save some love for me?'

'My heart is full, Sam. I love you.'

'And there are no impediments to us marrying soon? You won't have to leave now?'

She looked into his dark eyes, wondered why she still hesitated. He kissed her gently on her lips.

'You're still unsure?'

'Not about you, Sam. It's the house, I think. I know the truth, but the memories will take a little time to disappear.'

Suddenly a siren sounded, its wail echoing through the hills.

'Bush fires,' they said together.

Fear clutched at Eve's heart.

'It's OK. Thank goodness you're here with me where you'll be safe. I'll have to report to the fire station, but I'll leave a couple of men here.'

'I'm coming, too. I can operate the radios and phones, make myself useful at the station,' Eve protested.

In a frenzy of activity, Sam rounded up the workers. They piled into trucks and drove off, grim-faced, to the fire station, leaving clouds of dust in their wake.

'Thank goodness Weetangera is well protected,' he said, helping Eve into his four-wheel drive, 'but the Valley may be in danger. I should have made time to check the water pumps and spoutings.'

'You had more important things on your mind,' she said.

★   ★   ★

Eve and Sam stood on the hillside looking down over Banksia Valley. The long, dry spell of hot northerly winds was over. A cool breeze blew into their faces, bringing with it the pungent smell of light rain on spent fires and ash. Only the fireplaces of the house stood erect amongst the twisted iron and burned timbers.

They made their way slowly down to the property, picking a path through the blackened stubble, once yellowed grasses and a floor deep with fallen leaves.

'I hoped the greenery of the rhodo-dendrons and camellias around the house might protect it,' Sam said.

'I don't think anything could have saved it, Sam. It was meant. I feel it in my bones. I feel . . . ' She paused.

'What?'

'You'll laugh at me.'

'Honestly, I won't.'

'I feel as if Lucy knew I'd never be comfortable again in the house, so she took a box of heavenly matches and . . . '

Sam tossed back his head and laughed. She struck him on the arm.

'You promised you wouldn't laugh.'

He drew her into his arms.

'You're a funny kid, but if believing that makes you happy, I believe it one hundred per cent myself. In fact, I'm willing to wager Lucy threw petrol around the place before reaching for the matches, to be sure she did the job properly!'

She laughed this time.

'You won't get rid of me now, Sam.

I'm here for ever. Let's rebuild a house of our own, one we can love and raise our children in.'

He lifted her face to his and kissed her gently.

'You mean it?'

'I've never meant anything more.'

'Come on,' he said, taking her hand, 'let's see how many skips you can get out of a stone, now you're free.'

And, arms entwined, they made their way down to the dam.

THE END

We do hope that you have enjoyed reading this large print book.

Did you know that all of our titles are available for purchase?

We publish a wide range of high quality large print books including:
Romances, Mysteries, Classics
General Fiction
Non Fiction and Westerns

Special interest titles available in large print are:
The Little Oxford Dictionary
Music Book, Song Book
Hymn Book, Service Book

Also available from us courtesy of Oxford University Press:
Young Readers' Dictionary
(large print edition)
Young Readers' Thesaurus
(large print edition)

For further information or a free brochure, please contact us at:
Ulverscroft Large Print Books Ltd.,
The Green, Bradgate Road, Anstey,
Leicester, LE7 7FU, England.
Tel: (00 44) **0116 236 4325**
Fax: (00 44) **0116 234 0205**